Tomorrowland

Tomorr

STORIES BY:

Michael Cart

James Cross Giblin

Ron Koertge

Lois Lowry

Katherine Paterson

Rodman Philbrick

Jon Scieszka

Tor Seidler

Gloria Skurzynski

Jacqueline Woodson

owLand

10 STORIES ABOUT THE **FUTURE**

COMPILED BY
Michael Cart

SCHOLASTIC PRESS / NEW YORK

For my mother . . .
yesterday, today, and tomorrow. — M.C.

Library of Congress Cataloging-in-Publication Data
Tomorrowland: ten stories about the future / compiled by Michael Cart.
Summary: A collection of ten stories about the future, by such authors as Lois
Lowry, Katherine Paterson, and Jon Scieszka.
ISBN 0-590-37678-0
1. Science fiction, American. 2. Children's stories, American. [1. Science fiction.
2. Short stories.] I. Cart, Michael.   p. cm.
PZ5.T6235 1999   [Fic]—dc21   98-54832   CIP   AC

10 9 8 7 6 5 4 3 2 1   9/9 0/0 01 02 03

Printed in the U.S.A.   37
First edition, October 1999
Book design by David Caplan

*Several of the stories in this collection reflect the diversity of popular opinion as
to the effective date of the millennium; i.e., does it start on January 1, 2000 or — as
some assert — on January 1, 2001?*

CONTENTS

Introduction

Future *(fyoo'cher)* *[from Latin* futurus, *about to be]*
1. The indefinite time yet to come 2. Something that
will happen in time to come 3. A prospective
or expected condition, especially one considered with
regard to growth, advancement, or development
4. What will happen; what is going to be

Suppose you could see into the future, the landscape of that time and place I call "Tomorrowland." What would you do with your newfound knowledge? Would you try to change the shape of tomorrow? Or would you be resigned to your fate, instead, after realizing that this "gift" of foresight had robbed you of your capacity to wonder and rendered hope obsolete?

Maybe it's fortunate, after all, that we can't see the future. But so long as we're human, that infinite range of possibilities we call our lives will be an irresistible summons to the imagination. And I suspect that, in the long run, speculation will always be more exciting than certainty.

For a writer's imagination the future is especially tantalizing. As evidence of that, here is a collection of stories that came into being when ten authors were invited to create their personal, very individual visions of times to come.

The results are amazingly varied. In these stories, for example, you'll discover that the future is as distant as Mars and as close as your next heartbeat. It is light with laughter and dark with despair. It is something that has humbled us and invited us to wonder since the beginning of time. In "*Homo . . . sapiens?*" Jon Scieszka turns the clock all the way back to 33,001 B.C. It is there that he reveals the future through a group of cavemen behaving badly at a raucous New Year's Eve party. In "Night of the Plague" by James Cross Giblin, a young monk in the year 1,000 looks up at the night sky and wonders if the world is about to end. And a thousand years later a contemporary teenager asks the same question in my own story, "Starry, Starry Night."

Similarly, to Ron Koertge, Lois Lowry, Tor Seidler, and Jacqueline Woodson, it is not the past but the present, with its vexing problems — problems like alienation, dehumanizing change, environmental ruin, and the meaning of family — that will define a future that is no further away in time than tomorrow.

To Rodman Philbrick and Katherine Paterson the future is far more distant in time — and even more dire. For the worlds they envision are ones where technology rules and humans have lost the capacity to feel and, hence, to care. Minds have become wastelands and hearts are empty lots.

Gloria Skurzynski, whose allegory of Cain and Abel takes us on a voyage to Mars, shows us that — for good or for ill — in her future, the human heart will remain the same as it always has, regardless of the planet it inhabits.

Such different stories. Such different futures. Yet all of them contain the same implicit invitation to think about how the seeds of possibility we planted in the past and continue to sow in the present might blossom into the future.

All of them invite us to consider how choices we make today will help shape tomorrow in ways we can only imagine. When the future arrives, will we find that we were all co-creators of the time to come? And will we be proud . . . or will we be dismayed?

The possibilities in these stories invite your consideration. Or perhaps they will inspire you to seek answers of your own.

Welcome to Tomorrowland, where your future is waiting to be discovered.

— *Michael Cart*
January 1999

HOMO . . . SAPIENS?

Jon Scieszka

Encyclopedia Universalis: *For years the species* Homo sapiens *and* Homo neanderthalensis *existed side by side. Then quite suddenly, 35,000 years ago,* Homo neanderthalensis *disappeared abruptly from the fossil record.*

December 31, 33,001 B.C.

A man in nicely fitted animal skins stands before a crowd seated around the remains of a large feast. He is a tall man with a well-defined chin and fully developed cranium. He speaks.

"Cave-ladies and cave-gentlemen, thank you for coming out for this wonderful feast today. Special thanks to Og and his hunters for the bison steaks and mammoth kidneys. Delicious."

Hoots, claps, and the pounding of leftover bones by the happy diners.

"Thanks also to Neg and her decorating committee. Fabulous cave paintings. The Venus fertility figure centerpieces are just perfect."

More polite hooting, clapping, and smacking of bones.

"Tonight, as you know, we are celebrating putting the tenth rock in the tenth pouch in the tenth pile of rock pouches. And if you think that's a lot of rocks, you are right."

"That's a lot of rocks!" calls someone in the back near the fermented-grain drink bowl. Everyone laughs.

"And a lot of cycles of the Fire-in-the-Sky. One thousand cycles to be exact. So we have decided to call this momentous event . . . the Big Pile of Rocks. And now, on the eve of this auspicious occasion, our great chief and leader — Raga."

The speaker gestures toward a large man in reindeer antlers and pauses for a crowd cheer.

Crowd cheer.

"Our glorious leader, Raga, has asked me, as Tribal Spokesperson, to look back at who we've been as *Homo sapiens* in this last Big Pile and to look forward to who we can be as *Homo sapiens* in the next Big Pile."

"That's a lot of rocks!" from the voice in the back again. More crowd laughter.

"Thank you, Duh, for that witty observation. Which reminds me — why did the *Homo neanderthalensis* throw the rock off the cliff? He wanted to see time fly."

Crowd chuckle.

"But seriously, folks, we *Homo sapiens* have come a long way in the last thousand cycles. We are the species with upright posture, bipedal locomotion, and a skull with an average brain capacity of 1,350 cubic centimeters."

Heads nod. Bones and stones clap together.

"With our hands freed from that embarrassing ape-style knucklewalking, we've made snazzy tools, weapons, and art. We've rocked the world using both the power grip and the precision thumb and fingers grip. We *Homo sapiens* have made the opposable thumb what it is today, baby!"

Wild crowd hoots and yells. Much bone smacking, stone cracking, and weapon rattling. Several bloody injuries occur.

"And can we talk about what *Homo sapiens* have done with our revved-up cranial capacity? A social life. Religious beliefs. Superior organization and hunting skills. Thought! Speech! The ability to make and use symbols!"

The speaker raises one arm and points his index finger skyward.

"We are number one. We're number one! We're number ONE! WE'RE NUMBER ONE! WE'RE NUMBER . . ."

Crowd takes up a frenzied chant, dance, and weapon

display for the next half hour. A few of the smaller participants go down in the celebration.

"Yes, *Homo sapiens*. We are number one after this last Big Pile of Rocks. But where will we be in the next Big Pile?"

"Thas a lotta rocks!" from the voice in the back. A few scattered nervous laughs.

"We *Homo sapiens* are number one. One of two hundred different species of the primate order. And every one of those other species would just as soon eat you as look at you. Take the Neanderthals. I hear they don't worry about burying their dead . . . because they eat them!"

Groans and shouts of disgust and disapproval.

"And what's with those big brows, flat heads, and bowed legs? I know chimps who walk a straighter line. That's not human."

More uneasy shouts and murmurs.

"Did you hear what the Neanderthal said to the maggot chewing on the three-month-old mammoth carcass? 'You gonna finish that?'"

A relieved burst of rowdy laughter.

"That's the truth, you know. Neanderthals can't hunt anything bigger or smarter than themselves. So they're pretty much stuck with roots and berries and dead animals. Don't make any regular places to live like us *Homo sapiens*. Can't talk like us *Homo sapiens*. That's not human.

"So is this going to be a celebration of the last Big Pile

of Rocks? Or the next Big Pile of Rocks? We know where we've been. Where are we going?

"We are *Homo sapiens*, 'man the wise.' We can think.

"I think the only way to make it to the next Big Pile of Rocks is to get rid of the competition before they get rid of us. What do you think?"

The man raises his index finger once more.

"We're number one! We're number one! We're number one!" The chant dance builds again. A few men raise flaked, stone-tipped spears. Others pound clubs. Someone twirls an ax murderously overhead.

The reindeer-horned chief leads the frenzied crowd down to the Neanderthal camp on the river.

One man stays behind near the empty fermented-grain drink bowl. "*Homo sapiens?*" he says. "That's a lot of rocks."

Author's Note

As I thought about what people might become 1,000 years in the future, I began to wonder what people had been thousands of years in the past. Could they, back then, have imagined us now? What had changed from then to now? What had stayed the same?

Humans of every time and place have thought of themselves as the best and brightest thing in all creation. Even though, scientifically speaking, both cockroaches and crocodiles have been much more successful than us at surviving. Humans also seem to have the unstoppable urge to label anyone different from them as "wrong" or "evil." These seem to me the not-so-attractive human traits that have remained the same.

I remembered reading something about the mystery of Neanderthal man's disappearing suddenly from the fossil record. No one knows exactly what happened to Neanderthal man. We do know that another species of human lived at the same time. What I think happened to Neanderthal man is "Homo . . . sapiens?"

THE LAST BOOK IN THE UNIVERSE

Rodman Philbrick

If you're reading this, it must be a thousand years from now. Because nobody around here reads anymore. Why bother, when you can just probe it? Put all the images and excitement right inside your brain and let it rip. Trendies, shooters, sexbos — name it and you can probe it. Shooters are hot right now, but last year all anybody wanted to probe was a trendy.

Sexbos, they're *always* popular, even if nobody wants to admit it. Why that is, I can't say exactly, because I've never probed a sexbo or any of the other mindflicks. Not because I wouldn't like to, but because I've got this serious medical condition that means I'm allergic to electrode needle probes. Stick one of those in my brain and it'll kick off a really bad seizure and then — total meltdown, lights out, that's all, folks.

Which really borks me. Because I'd love to probe a sexbo, if you want to know the truth. Just so I'd know what everybody else is talking about.

They call me Spaz, which is kind of a mope name, but I don't mind, not anymore. I'm talking into an old voicewriter program that prints out my words, because I was there when the Bully Bangers went to wheel the Ryter, and I saw what they saw, and I heard what they heard, and it kind of turned my brain around.

See, the Ryter was this old geez living in a little stackbox on the edge of the projos. A place where losers get stored, because they can't get anything better. Nobody owns the stackboxes, and if you squat in one long enough, I guess you can call it home — if home is a ten-by-ten concrete box stacked ten high, in rows of a hundred. Used to use 'em for prisons, before they came up with the mind fix for criminals.

There's no hydro in the stacks, no plumbing, no broadband, no nothing. Just the empty box and a door that looks like the lid on a sideways dumpster. Which seems fitting for the human garbage that lives there. Mostly can't-copers and won't-workers and assorted needlebrains. Which is what the Bully Bangers thought the Ryter was, until he showed them different.

Wheeling a geez means slow-dragging him from behind a jetbike so the righteous can see what a loser he is and have their fun, which is normally fatal. The Bully Bangers do it all the time, just for the cool of it. I'm not officially down with the Bangers, but they let me hang some, and now and then they throw me a bone, like maybe a bust-down or a rip. A bustdown is when you bust down the door and take what you want. A rip is like a mugging in the backtimes, before the words got shorter and the world got meaner.

That's how I met the Ryter, when the Bully Bangers said I could bust down his box. Not that I expected to find anything cherry. The geezers who live in the stacks don't have much worth stealing. But I didn't have anything better to do, and when the Bangers give you something you take it, or they might wheel you, just for the giggle and spark of it.

Anyhow, back to the old geez. The first thing that was different about him was he left his door open. See, I'm all jacked to kick the mutha down, but when I turn the corner the door is open, and my foot connects with nothing, just empty air. Which makes me feel like a real googan, and I guess he saw the look of it on my face.

"Could have happened to anybody," the geez says. He's

kneeling on the floor by some old crate he'd fixed up as a desk, and he doesn't seem the least surprised about the bustdown. "Come on in," he goes, "make yourself at home."

I go, "Huh?" like, what are you, twisted? You *want* a bustdown? You *want* to get ripped? Are you mindsick or what? Except all I really say is "Huh?" because the rest is implied, which is a word I later got from the Ryter.

"I heard about the Bully Bangers giving me up," he says, like it's no big deal. "Bound to happen sooner or later. Help yourself, son. Everything of value is over there in the corner."

He points out a gimme tote bag with a few crumball items inside. An old clock alarm vidscreen, a baseball mitt so old it isn't molded plastic, a coffee machine with the cord all neat and coiled. It doesn't amount to much, but there's enough for a few credits at the pawn mart. Better than usual for the stacks.

"Go on," he says. "Take it."

Normally I would, but there's something not normal about the whole situation. Like the way he coiled up the cord to the coffeemaker. You know you're going to get ripped, and you do that? Is it some kind of trick or what?

It's like he knows what I'm thinking, because the next thing he says is, "This isn't my first bustdown. Just thought I'd make it easier for us both."

"What else you got?" I say, closing in on the geez.

He smiles at me, which makes his old wrinkled face sort of glow, in a weird way. Like he wants an excuse to smile, no matter what happens. "What makes you think I've got anything else?" he asks, kind of craftylike.

That's when I see there are stacks of paper under the crate, and he's been sitting there in front of them, hoping I wouldn't notice. "What's this?" I go.

"Nothing of value," he says. "Just a book, if you want to know."

I scoff at him and snarl, "Liar! Books are in libraries. Or they used to be."

He starts to say something and then he stops, like I've given him something important to think about. "Hmmm," he goes. "You're aware that books used to be in libraries. That was before you were born, so how did you know?"

I shrug and go, "I heard is all. When I was a little kid. About how things used to be before the badtimes."

"And you remember everything you hear?"

"Pretty much," I say. "Doesn't everybody?"

The old geez chuckles. "Not hardly. Most of 'em, they've had their brains softened by probes and mind-flicks, and they can't really retain much. Long-term memory is a thing of the past, no pun intended. The only ones left who can remember are a few old geezers like me. And, apparently, you."

Now that I think about it, I know what he's talking

about. I've always had a lot of old stuff in my head that everybody else seems to have forgotten.

"What else do you remember?" the geez asks.

"What do you care?" I say.

The geez gives me a look, like he wants to memorize me or something. "That's what I do," he says. "I remember and I write it down. I take other people's memories, and I write those down, too. Of course, I change things to fit the story, but that's all part of the process."

"Process? You mean like a word processor?"

For some reason he finds that amusing. "Not exactly. Instead of using a computer to process the words, I do it directly. From my head to the page, writing down the words by hand, like they did in the backtimes. Of course, I used to use a voicewriter like everybody else, but it got ripped a couple of bustdowns ago. So now I do it this way," he says, showing me the stacks of paper covered with pen scratching. "Primitive, but it works."

"Yeah," I go. "You're doing it. But what are you doing?"

"Writing a book," he says. "The story of my life. The story of everybody's life, and the way things were when there used to be books."

"Nobody reads books anymore," I tell him.

He nods sadly. "I know. But someday that may change. And if and when it does, they'll want to know what happened, and why. They'll want stories that don't come out of a mindprobe needle. They'll want to read books again, someday."

"They?" I go. "Who do you mean?"

"Those who will be alive at some future date," he says.

Those who will be alive at some future date. I don't know why, but the way he says it gives me a shiver. Because I'd never thought about the future. You want to be down with the Bully Bangers, you can't think about the future. There's only room for the right here and the want-it-now. The future is like the moon. You never expect to go there or think about what it might be like. What's the point if you can't touch it or steal it?

"What's your story?" the geez asks, like he really wants to know.

I go, "I don't have a story."

Almost before I get the words out, he's shaking his head, like he knew what I was going to say and can't wait to disagree. "Everybody has a story," he says. "There are things about your life that are specific only to you. Secrets you know."

Finally the old geez is starting to make sense. And there's something about him I sort of like — or anyhow something I don't hate — so I sit there and listen to him jabber on about his book and all the stories and secrets he's been writing down for years, since before his hair went white and he got old. Stuff about before the badtimes and how we all used to be so rich we'd throw stuff away after using it once, and that's how the world got used up. Stuff about how there used to be shiny things called stars in the sky, before the smog got permanent.

The way he tells it, he makes me see it all inside my head, even the things called stars.

"You've never seen green grass," he says with a sigh. "Or smelled it. Standing outside on a summer night with your eyes closed, just smelling the grass. It made you glad to be alive. Glad enough so you didn't need to stick needles in your brain."

"I don't stick needles in my brain. I can't."

The old geez looks righteously surprised. "You can't? Why not?"

I don't know what, but there was something about the Ryter that made me want to tell him about my medical condition. Mostly I'm fine, but every now and then I spaz out.

"Caesar's disease!" the Ryter says with a sparkle in his eyes.

I go, "Who?"

"Julius Caesar. He conquered the world a long time ago. His life inspired many stories and plays. His fame lasted for more than two thousand years, until people stopped reading."

"And he was a spaz like me? You expect me to believe that?"

"Yes," the old geez said. "I do."

The funny thing is, I did believe him.

Anyhow, what happened is I left without taking anything, and when I came back the next day it was like the Ryter was expecting me.

"I've been thinking about you, Spaz. About how you

can still remember things. Every writer needs a reader. I figured my reader wasn't even born yet, but here you are."

I figure he must be making fun of me. "You think I care about those scratches you make on paper? Is that what you think?"

It's like there's an angry thing inside me that wants to bust out and hurt something, and right now what it wants to hurt is the old geezer, for laughing at me.

But his voice isn't laughing when he says, "I can teach you to read. That's not a problem. I'd like to teach you, if you'll let me. With a mind like yours — a mind that remembers — it won't take that long. A year or so, that's all. Maybe less."

That's when I go ahead and tell him the real secret, the one I didn't want to tell him yesterday. "You haven't got a year. The Bully Bangers are going to wheel you."

"You're sure about that?" he asks, looking worried. "I thought it was just another bustdown. I can handle getting ripped off, but I'll never survive getting dragged behind a jetbike."

Something makes me tell him, "You got to run away. Save yourself. Now, before it's too late."

The old geez sighs and looks at me with his soft eyes. "I'm too old to run. My running days are over." He thinks about something for a while, and I'm waiting because I know whatever it is, it's important. "I've got a better idea," he says. "You finish my book. Make it your own book."

"What? Are you zoomed?"

"I'm quite serious," he says. "You've got a brain, son, and the ability to remember. Two essentials for a writer. You're an outsider, and that's good, too, because outsiders tend to pay attention. And it helps that you're young and strong, because writing takes strength and perseverance. It also takes courage, and you've got plenty of that."

Which is a wacked thing to say. I ask how he knows I've got courage.

"Because you're not afraid to listen," he says.

"But I can't even read," I say. "How can I write?"

"You'll figure it out," the Ryter says. "It doesn't matter how the words get on the page, just so they do."

He's starting to tell me about the old voicewriter programs when all of a sudden the Bully Bangers come for him. I hadn't expected them quite this soon, but here they are, swarming through the stacks like wild things. Shrieking and laughing and screaming all at the same time.

"Save my pages!" the old geez begs me as they come through the open door and grab him.

I want to, but the Bangers see that the bundles of old paper mean something to the geez, and so they tear the pages to shreds and burn them. They dance in the paper fire, kicking and howling and biting each other, because they're hungry for blood and they can't wait.

As they're tying a rope around the Ryter and hooking it to the back of the jetbike, he calls to me. "Quick!" he says. "I'll have to tell you the rest of the book. All you have to do is remember. Later you can write it down."

"Let him go!" I tell the Bangers, but they're not listening. They can't listen, they don't know how.

"Forget it!" the Ryter says as they fire up the cycle. "Too late for me. But you must listen and remember!"

And so I follow as they wheel him through the stacks and the projos. Gunning the jetbike extra loud to draw a crowd, pulling him along just fast enough so he keeps falling down and getting dragged behind. It doesn't seem to matter how bad it gets or how much it hurts, the Ryter keeps on telling me what's in the book and why it's important to remember.

"We live and we die!" he shouts. "That's what it all comes down to. That's what it is to be human. Life and death, Spaz! Go for the big picture!"

For some reason it's me he's counting on. Because the Bangers have taken away everything, and all he's got left is what he remembers about his book.

"Find people who care!" he groans as he's dragged through the broken rubble of the streets. "They still exist. Listen to their stories. Write them down. Put in the good parts, but don't forget the bad. Because the bad informs the good."

He's shouting to be heard over the roar of the jetbike, and I'm running along, trying to keep up, trying to hold all his words in my head. "Every great book is about the mystery of life, Spaz! Why are we here? Why are we born? You won't find all the answers, but you have to keep asking the questions!"

A couple of times I try to grab him and undo the drag ropes, but the Bangers keep shoving me off. They think it's funny, me trying to free a wheeler. Part of the game. Their eyes are dead cold because they can't feel anything, and I know if I'm not careful, they'll wheel me, too.

"Don't risk it!" the Ryter warns me when I make a move. "You're my only hope."

"But I can't stop them!" I scream, running after the jetbike, watching his frail body spin on the rope. I'm not sure why, but my eyes are filled with tears.

"Remember my book!" he cries with his bloody mouth. "You're my only hope. Live and remember!"

People all over the projos have come out to see what's going down. Wheelers are mostly quiet. Sometimes they moan or scream a little, but never for long. The Ryter, he's the exception, and they don't know what to make of some old geez shouting out stories while they drag him to death. And to make it even more wacked, he sounds almost cheerful, like he's pleased to have an audience at last.

"Everybody has a story!" he chokes out as the rope gets tighter and the engines rev higher. "All you have to do is listen! You're my hope for the future, son! You're the only one left! You're the last book in the universe!"

The Bangers finally get bored and decide to end it. They gun their engines hard and drag the life out of him until there's nothing left. Nothing but silence, and the stink of jetbike fumes, and the bundle of rags and bones that used to be the Ryter.

I didn't stay until the very end. When the Ryter finally stopped telling his stories I ran away. I ran to the river, but there were dead things floating there, so I ran to the tallest building in the projos and climbed out on the roof and watched the sky, hoping maybe I'd see the shiny things called stars.

I never did.

Later that night I did a really strange thing. I went down to the pawn mart and found this old voicewriter in the tronic junk pile, covered with dust. There's a lot of gizmos you have to attach, but basically you talk in one end and words come out the other. And so I started talking about the Ryter and what he told me about the stars and grass and stuff, and what happened to him when the Bully Bangers came, and what he said when he was dying.

I didn't know it then, but I'd started writing a book. It's not the Ryter's book exactly, because he never got the chance to tell me the whole thing. It's a story that started out with the Ryter, and now it grows inside my head. The story of everything I see and hear. I'm putting in all the people I know, the ones I love and the ones I hate, and everything that happens, the good and the bad, the struggle for life and the struggle for death, everything. Now that I've started I can't stop writing, because like the old geez said, I'm the last book in the universe.

Until you read me, that is.

Author's Note

When I was asked to submit a story for this anthology, I knew at once that the tale would take place in the future. After all, I came of age reading authors like Ray Bradbury, Isaac Asimov, and Ursula Le Guin, who wrote about future worlds in a way that made me want to be an author when I grew up. Of course as anyone who knows me is well aware, I never actually grew up. My brain is still twelve years old — and that's a good thing, because the twelve-year-old brain is highly imaginative and fascinated by new ideas.

For me, inventing a new story often starts with the "what if" game. I'd already decided my tale would take place in a future world. But what about that future world? What if there came a time when no one read books? What if *books and the whole concept of reading had been forgotten? What would the world be like? What would the people be like?*

I didn't have any answers, but I knew someone who did: a young man named Spaz. I wanted Spaz to be an outsider, a kid from the wrong side of the tracks — if they have tracks in the future, that is. The world he inhabits is a tough place. Basically you're either down with one of the gangs or you're a victim, and Spaz doesn't like to think of himself as a victim. But there's something special about Spaz, and that's his ability to feel empathy for someone who is his victim: the eccentric old man called "The Ryter."

When I finished the story I didn't want to stop, which is always a good sign when you're writing a story. As a matter of fact, I didn't stop. Spaz has more to say — a whole novel's worth of more — and so I'm taking notes, putting his words down on paper, and making a book about a world where there are no books.

See you there. And you better bring something to read.

WHAT'S THE POINT?

Tor Seidler

On a breezy Sunday in late August, Mrs. Fury announced at the breakfast table that it was the perfect day for testing the latest models of runabout sailboats. She and Mr. Fury owned and operated Keller Bay Sporting Goods.

"But you said we were going to the carnival!" cried Louise.

"That's true," said Mr. Fury, who didn't really care for sailing.

"But I'll need you to put up the jib, dear," said Mrs. Fury. "Jarred'll take you, Lou. Won't you, Jarred?"

"I don't know, Mom," said Jarred.

The carnival had been a blast the previous night with his buddies from the football team, but the idea of going with his ten-year-old sister was less than thrilling.

"Only till two — then Lou has Jenny Finch's birthday party to go to." Mrs. Fury slipped Jarred a twenty-dollar bill. "Here, bring home some more loot."

The money swayed him, and an hour later he and Louise were making the rounds at the carnival, which stopped in Keller Bay for a few days at the end of every summer. They had gone through about half the money when they walked up to the Moon Shot booth.

"No way, kid," said the burly man behind the counter. "I had it up to here with you last night."

"But my sister can try, can't she?" Jarred said.

The man sized Louise up and grunted.

"What do you do?" asked Louise.

"See them holes, sweetheart?" The man pointed to the booth's backdrop, about forty feet away. It was painted like a starry night, with three holes in it. The hole labeled SUN was a little more than a foot in diameter, the EARTH hole around ten inches, MOON about seven inches. "You get two tries," he said. "SUN gets you one of these." He flicked his eyes up at a flock of stuffed animals — little yellow ducks — hanging from the ceiling. "EARTH, you get yer choice of them guys." The man cocked his head at the side wall, where a school of dolphins, twice the size of the ducks, mingled with a herd of penguins. "MOON gets you a grand prize." On the other side wall, things like a set of knives, a toaster, an electric drill, a clock radio, an electric shaver, and bottles of fancy perfume were spaced out on shelves. "Least what's left of 'em," he added, giving Jarred a sour look. "If I'd known you was the big star quarterback, I wouldn't have let you keep going. Just you look too young."

"This is where you got my high-speed modem?" Louise asked.

"Yup," said Jarred. The "loot" he'd brought home had also included a blender and a set of socket wrenches for his parents and a Walkman for himself.

He plunked down two quarters, and the man handed Louise a football, which she set on the counter while she cleaned her thick glasses on her Surf the Net T-shirt. On her first throw, the ball arced up almost to the ceiling and, on its way down, smacked the Big Dipper. Her second try wasn't even a spiral, though the wobbling ball did hit the backdrop only a few inches from the EARTH hole.

"Darn," she said. "I wanted a dolphin."

"Next year, when your hand's bigger," Jarred said.

"Tell you what, Mr. QB," the man said. "Do a moonie on one go, and she gets a dolphin."

The diameter of the football was only about an inch less than that of the MOON hole. Jarred licked the tips of the fingers on his right hand, picked up the ball, cocked his arm, and fired.

"You got an agent, kid?" the man said, handing Louise a dolphin.

From the Moon Shot they proceeded to the Spook House, which didn't spook even Louise. Then they had hot dogs and lemonade in the food tent. That left two dollars, just enough for a ride apiece. Jarred used his on the Double Cigar, which was more or less the equivalent of being strapped into a barrel tumbling down Niagara Falls. Afterward, he leaned dizzily on a fence while Louise rode the Ferris wheel.

"How's it going?"

Jarred turned to a boy a couple of years older than he was: sixteen, maybe, or seventeen. The stranger had broad shoulders, aviator sunglasses with mirrored lenses, and spiky hair bleached almost white by the sun.

"Not bad," Jarred said. "You?"

"Not bad — considering."

"Considering what?"

"That there's a hole the size of Greenland in the ozone layer."

Jarred laughed.

"B. J. Fox," the older boy said, extending a hand.

"Jarred Fury," Jarred said, shaking.

"Nice to meet you, Jerry."

"No, Jarred," Jarred said, a little taken aback.

Keller Bay wasn't a very big town, so the middle school and high school were combined, and last fall Jarred had become the first eighth-grade starting quarterback in the school's varsity football history. In fact, as far as anyone knew, the first eighth-grade starting quarterback in the history of the state — maybe even the country. So he was kind of used to people knowing his name.

"Sorry — Jarred," B. J. Fox said.

"Where you from?"

"L.A."

"Los Angeles?"

"No, Lost Atlantis."

Jarred laughed again, this time blushing a bit. "What are you doing in Delaware?"

"We moved here about a month ago. My old man's a scientist. DuPont hired him."

"Were you here last night?" Jarred asked, thinking he might have seen a guy with bleached hair in the crowd that had gathered when he was cleaning out the Moon Shot.

"At this two-bit gig? Once is plenty."

"What's two-bit about it?"

"Compared to Magic Mountain. Or Disneyland."

"I guess Keller Bay must seem kind of small after Los — after L.A."

"Yeah, but the air's better. Still doomed, though."

"What do you mean?"

"It's at sea level."

"So?"

"Global warming. When the ice caps melt, this burg'll be for your pal." B. J. pointed his chin at the dolphin, which Louise had entrusted to Jarred's care.

"It's not mine," Jarred said, embarrassed. "But even if the ice caps melt, it won't be for centuries."

"Wouldn't bet on it. Anyhow, what's the diff?"

"What do you mean?"

"You don't want to know."

"Who says?"

"Well, if you want to hear my time theory, it'll take a while. What are you doing tomorrow afternoon?"

"Football practice. Two-a-days start tomorrow."

B. J. smiled as if at a private joke.

"You don't like football?"

"It's okay, if you don't have anything better to do."

"What's better than football?"

"In this heat and humidity? Did you know the life expectancy of a football player's eight years less than the national average? But then, what's eight years, right?"

"Eight years? That's, like, my whole school life."

"You going into eighth?"

"Ninth," Jarred said, straightening up. "What about you?"

"Be a junior."

The Ferris wheel's brakes began to screech, and soon Louise came running up. Jarred wasn't sorry to have her take the stuffed animal off his hands.

"It was great!" she said. "From the top you can see Chesapeake Bay."

"Home of the red tides," B. J. murmured.

"Um, Lou, this is B. J. Fox. He just moved here from L.A."

"What's a red tide?" Louise asked.

"Pollution. Kills the shellfish. But hey, the ocean's not totally wrecked yet. Our house is on the beach. You guys want to come for a swim?"

"I've got to go to Jenny Finch's birthday party," Louise said.

"How about you, man? You can ride on the back of my baby."

"Your baby?"

B. J. pointed at a resplendent red-and-black motorcycle on the edge of the parking lot.

"That's yours?" Jarred said, gaping.

"I know, it eats fossil fuel. But it gets a hundred miles to the gallon — and I figure, what's the diff? It'll all be gone in fifty years anyway. You up for it?"

"Sure," said Jarred, highly flattered that an older boy from L.A. — with his own motorcycle, no less — would want to hang out with him. "We can drop by our house and pick up my suit."

Jarred and his sister took after their parents: Jarred after their mother, Louise after their father. In her younger days Mrs. Fury had been a champion field hockey and tennis player, and at Keller Bay Sporting Goods she was the one who kept abreast of the latest running shoes, the latest graphite-shafted golf clubs, the latest scuba gear and snowboards. Mr. Fury loved numbers: in *his* younger days he'd gone around with a slide rule in a leather sheath attached to his belt, like a knight with his sword, though he'd long since transferred his affections to calculators and computers. It was he who kept the business' accounts and dealt with taxes, employees' salaries, invoices, etc.

On the way home from the store on Monday, Mr. and Mrs. Fury stopped at Gino's and picked up a couple of pizzas: a large onion and mushroom for them and Louise and a medium pepperoni just for Jarred. Jarred was a major pepperoni pizza fan.

But not that evening.

"Aren't you hungry, son?" said Mr. Fury.

The four of them were eating at the kitchen table. At least Mr. and Mrs. Fury and Louise were eating. Jarred was just toying with his food.

"Not really," he said in an oddly expressionless voice.

"But didn't you work up an appetite at football practice?" Mrs. Fury asked.

"He didn't go," said Louise.

"What!" said Mrs. Fury. "Are you sick?"

"Not really," he said in the same lifeless tone.

And so it went all week long. Coach Gleason and Jarred's buddies from the football team called so often to find out when he was coming to practice that he quit answering the phone. On Thursday, Mrs. Fury knocked off work early and dragged him to see Dr. Shue.

"Summer vacationitis," Dr. Shue told her privately after examining the boy. "I've always maintained that summer vacation goes on too long. Kids get bored. He'll come around in a couple of weeks, when school starts. We're all counting on him for an undefeated season!"

"But he won't even go to practice."

"Jarred doesn't need practice. He's a natural."

"But if he doesn't go, he won't even make the team."

"Well, all I can tell you is he's fine. A little underweight, but healthy as a horse."

"He barely eats. I end up giving his dinner to Henry."

"Henry who?"

"Our dog. According to Louise, all he does is stare at reruns all day."

"Your dog watches TV?"

"No, Jarred."

"Ah. Well, like I said, summer vacation's just too darn long."

The one sport Mr. Fury actually liked was hiking, and every year he and the family spent Labor Day week walking a new section of the Appalachian Trail. As a boy, Mr. Fury had memorized the height of every major peak in the mountain range; his goal was to check them all off his mental list. (So far, he'd climbed a combined 123,781 feet.) Mrs. Fury always enjoyed the hike, too — and later on, when customers came into the store wanting hiking gear, she could say things like, "This tent won't leak even in a downpour, I can guarantee it," or, "I can tell you from personal experience that these boots have the best traction money can buy."

For the past two years, Jarred had missed the family outing because of football practice. But since he didn't seem interested in practice this year, his mother tried to convince him to come along.

"It'll get you out of the dumps, honey," she said, standing in his bedroom doorway the night before their departure. "Think of all that fresh mountain air and those panoramic views!"

"It'll just depress me," he said in his new, dead voice. He was lying on his bed in wrinkled clothes, staring dully at a water spot on the ceiling.

"Why's that?"

"It'll just remind me how it's all being destroyed."

"What do you mean, honey?"

"It'll all end up as housing developments."

"That's ridiculous."

"Wait and see."

After brushing her teeth, Louise paid him a visit, too.

"Come with us, Jarred."

"I don't feel like it, Lou."

"You're not just going to lie there the whole time, are you?"

"I might."

"You won't forget to feed Henry, will you?"

"What's the point, Lou?"

"What do you mean? You want him to starve? What do you have against Henry all of a sudden?"

"Nothing. Just, pets depress me."

"Why?"

"Because in a hundred years they're the only animals that'll be around."

"Why's that?"

"There'll be so many billions of people, there won't be any habitats for wild animals left. So the only ones'll be a bunch of lousy cats and dogs and cows and a few parakeets and hamsters."

Later, when Mr. and Mrs. Fury stopped by to say good night, Jarred was still staring at the water spot.

"Will you start the jalopy once or twice for me, son?" Mr. Fury said. "She's been a little cranky lately." They were taking the Astro Van but leaving Mr. Fury's beloved vintage Chevy, which had 176,451 miles on the odometer.

"If I have to," Jarred sighed.

"I thought you loved starting the car. I thought you were counting the months till you can get your learner's permit."

"What's the point?" he said.

"What do you mean?"

"By the middle of the next century we'll have used up all the oil. Do you know how long it takes for oil to form?"

"Um, 2.36 million years, I believe — on the average."

"Exactly! And in one measly century we've burned up more than half the earth's supply!"

"Well, honey," said Mrs. Fury, "you won't forget to water the lawn and the garden, will you?"

"I'll try to remember. But I don't really see the point."

"What do you mean?"

"I mean, the sun's just going to die out, and then there won't be any more photosynthesis, and all life on Earth'll wither up. What's the point of keeping things going when the end's inevitable?"

"But son," said Mr. Fury, "I read that the sun won't burn out for at least 5.7434 billion years. In 5.7434 billion years, I really doubt any of us are going to be around to care."

"Think about it, Dad. What's the difference between five billion years and five seconds?"

"Well, five seconds is — one-Mississippi, two-Mississippi, three-Mississippi, four-Mississippi, five-Mississippi. Whereas five billion years is considerably longer."

"But that's just a *quantitative* difference. I'm talking about *qualitative*."

"Qualitative," his mother said thoughtfully. "You mean because they're both intervals of time?"

"Bingo! And what does time always do?"

"Well, it always passes, I guess."

"Bingo again, Mom. You're . . . "

"Not as stupid as you thought?"

"No, I was just going to say . . . " He sighed again. "I'll do the watering. Even though it's a fool's game."

"Well, don't forget to eat. The freezer's full of frozen dinners. Promise?"

"I'll try and remember," he said, rolling over onto his stomach.

This year's stretch of the Appalachian Trail was in West Virginia. On the drive there, Louise climbed up between her parents in the front seat of the Astro Van so they could discuss Jarred without shouting.

"I know what he's going through," Mr. Fury said. "I was about his age when I learned about irrational numbers. I was down for days."

"I was just his age when I lost to Ginny Fibbs in sixteen-and-unders," Mrs. Fury said, "six-three, six-one. That was the day my Wimbledon dreams died. I shuffled around like a zombie the rest of the summer."

"But Jarred didn't lose at anything," Louise said. "And he doesn't even care about math. I think it's the red-tide guy from the carnival."

"What red-tide guy?" Mrs. Fury said.

"He called himself B. J. Fox. I'm sure he filled Jarred's head with all these crazy ideas."

"Come to think of it," Mr. Fury said, "that quantitative/qualitative stuff really didn't sound like him."

"And missing football practice isn't like him, either," said Mrs. Fury. "But I'm sure it's just a phase. By the time we get back, he'll be his old self."

When they got back to Keller Bay a week (and 18,341 combined mountain feet) later, Jarred was lying on the living room sofa staring up at a cobweb in a corner of the ceiling. The three hikers had radiant tans, but he looked like a ghost. And though his only exercise had been to go up and down the stairs a couple of times a day (there'd been two soaking rains, so he hadn't even had to go out to water the garden), he'd actually lost eight pounds. Of the fifteen frozen dinners Mrs. Fury had stocked the freezer with, only three had been eaten.

Mr. Fury headed straight out to Gino's to get a pepperoni pizza to tempt him. Mrs. Fury headed straight up to the master bedroom to have a private phone conversation with Dr. Shue. Louise, separated from her computer for a full seven days, headed straight up to her room to surf the Internet with her new high-speed modem.

By slipping pizza slices under the table to Henry, Jarred fooled his parents into thinking he'd regained his appetite. Still, his mother declared that she was coming home the next day at lunchtime to take him to see Dr. Shue.

"He's got a golf game in the morning, but he promises to be back in the office by noon. I'll pick you up at ten of. Okay?"

"If you insist," Jarred said.

"But, honey, don't you want to feel better?"

"What's the point? I'm going to die in the long run anyway. We all are."

"Boy, it sure is nice to be home," Mr. Fury said.

Half an hour after Mr. and Mrs. Fury left for the store the next morning, Louise burst into Jarred's room.

"What's the matter, Lou?" Jarred said, rolling over languidly in bed. He was still in his wrinkled clothes, not having bothered to change into his pajamas.

"I'm blind!" she cried.

"What do you mean?"

"I broke my other glasses!"

"What do you mean, your other glasses?"

"I broke one pair on the hike. I just broke the other in the sink. Now I'm blind!"

"You're better off. Everywhere you look things are just falling apart."

"You've got to take me to the optician."

"I'm not going anywhere."

"Well, if I get run over on the way, it'll be your fault."

"Where is it?"

"Grove Street."

"There aren't any stores on Grove Street."

"Shows what you know. Anyway, I'm going to try and make it. They have my prescription there."

Louise turned to leave, but instead of going through the doorway she bumped into the wall.

"Okay, okay, let me put some shoes on," Jarred said, sitting up with a sigh.

The optician wasn't actually on Grove Street, but Keller Bay High-Middle School was. And though Louise really was all but blind without her glasses, she could tell by the whistles and thumping shoulder pads when they were walking by the football field.

"My shoe's untied," she said, letting go of her brother's arm.

While she crouched, Jarred peered through the chain-link fence at football practice: at the purple-and-gold helmets agleam in the morning sun, the pigskins spiraling into the blue sky, the tackles and guards and centers smashing into the blocking sled, with Coach Gleason riding on the back, barking commands. After untying and tying a shoelace, Louise finally stood up.

"Football practice?" she asked innocently.

"Stupid waste of energy," Jarred muttered, leading her away.

In half a block, Louise stopped with a sigh. "You know, Jarred, I lied to you," she said, reaching into her pocket. She pulled out her glasses, which weren't broken at all, and after wiping the lenses on her T-shirt, she put them on. But her brother wasn't even looking at her. He was staring off at the school parking lot.

"Jarred?"

He pointed. Parked between the bike rack and the flag-pole on the edge of the lot was a gleaming red-and-black motorcycle.

Jarred did an abrupt about-face and marched up the sidewalk, so fast Louise had to jog to keep up. When they got back to where she'd stopped to tie her shoe, he peered through the chain-link fence, seeking out the first-string offensive unit. He identified his buddies by the numbers on their practice jerseys: Freddy Miles, 45; Big John Billingsgate, the fullback, 32; his erstwhile favorite receiver, Paolo Forunata, 85. As he watched, a guy with his number — 11 — arced a pass to Paolo, who made a fingertip catch in the far end zone. A tuft of bleached blond hair was poking out the back of number 11's helmet.

"I talked to a bunch of kids from Los Angeles on the Internet late last night," Louise said. "There was one from a high school called Westwood who knew B. J. Fox. He made first-string quarterback his sophomore year there."

This got Jarred to look at her. "Why didn't you tell me?"

"I thought you might not believe me. You seemed so out of it I thought you'd have to see for yourself."

"Hey. Your glasses."

She laughed. "That's what I was just telling you. I lied."

He turned slowly back to football practice. "But he . . ."

"What? Fed you all that stuff about time and dying and pollution?"

"On the beach. While you were at Jenny's birthday party."

Suddenly he remembered thinking he'd noticed a boy with bleached blond hair in the crowd the night he was cleaning out the Moon Shot. B. J. Fox must have seen how good he was and hit on a plan to get him out of the way.

"Talk about being blind!" Jarred cried, giving the chain-link fence a swift kick. "I'm going to kill that guy!"

"Oh, don't do that," Louise said. "Just beat him out for first string. The lockers are over there, right? You could be suited up in five minutes."

The longer Jarred stared off at the offensive unit, the narrower his eyes got, and Louise had a good idea that his concern about the future was narrowing as well — to the here and now.

"Go ahead, Jarred. I'll be fine."

Her brother turned back to her, and for the first time in two weeks he cracked a smile.

Author's Note

I suppose "What's the Point?" stems from two adolescent memories. One is of traveling carnivals. I always loved the colorful, seedy atmosphere of those transient little worlds that plunked themselves down for two or three days on the edge of town. Like most kids, I also loved the rides — the wilder the better — and the shooting galleries, etc., with the seductive prizes. Though "What's the Point?" is meant to be a comic story, the other memory it's based on is of adolescent existential despair, the feeling that comes along with self-awareness that life itself is as impermanent and insubstantial as one of those carnivals: here today maybe, but gone tomorrow.

HIS BROTHER'S KEEPER

Gloria Skurzynski

Six months is a long time to be sealed up inside a tin can. That's what their father said. He was joking about the tin can — *Adventurer* was the most sophisticated spaceship ever designed. Big enough to hold the 1322 pounds of oxygen for breathing; the twenty tons of water for bathing, drinking, and cleaning; the one-plus ton of food needed to sustain a crew of four on the way to Mars. Or in this case, a *family* of four.

The Holbrooks weren't the first

humans to make the trip to Mars, but they were the first family unit: mother Janine, a propulsion engineer; father Stewart, an exobiologist with a PhD in chemistry; son Kern, fifteen, a mathematical genius; and son Dylan, thirteen, a — well, so far, no one knew for sure just what Dylan was. Except that, among other things, he liked to fiddle with the green, growing plants that sucked up most of the carbon dioxide the Holbrooks exhaled.

"It's not just the fresh crop of salad every ten days to go with our freeze-dried pizza," Dylan said, smiling. "It's more. Plants are *alive*. It's like they're part of the crew."

"Oh, sure." Kern was used to his brother's quirky notions. Dylan usually dreamed away his days. Not Kern. Kern studied, all the way to Mars. He'd started cramming even before *Adventurer* launched, right after the biggest news in the history of mankind got announced.

"Breakthrough!" he'd screamed, slamming into their Earth house while his parents packed the last few personal belongings they were allowed to take to Mars. "Did you hear it? Mom! Dad! Zero-point energy. They figured it out!"

His parents had been properly thrilled, but Dylan just said, "Oh, that."

"Don't give me *'Oh that'!*" Kern yelled, then carefully modulated his voice to say, "Now they can convert matter into energy, Dylan. That means — travel outside our solar system! To the nearest star." Kern rarely made the mistake of yelling at his brother, or at anyone. The Evaluators were always listening.

"Okay," Dylan had answered, "but first we're going to Mars. You and me and Mom and Dad."

Yeah, Mars. Suddenly the journey Kern had been anticipating with so much excitement lost its luster, because the future would now hold a bigger — a truly monumental — quest. People had been to Mars before. But no one had ever before flown to a star.

Zero-point energy would make it work. Physicists had just proved that there is no such thing as mass — only electric charge and energy, which together create the illusion of mass. All the while the Holbrooks traveled to Mars in the *Adventurer*, Kern studied the works of those physicists, learning how to expand the volume of space-time behind a starship while compressing it up ahead. In other words, how to propel a ship ever closer to the speed of light.

"Can't talk, Dylan," he kept saying as he studied during the long trip to Mars. In ten years, Kern would be twenty-five, just the right age to set forth on a voyage to the closest star, which would last twenty years each way. Kern knew he could stand the isolation, could deal with the unknown, and he knew he'd already made himself a prime candidate for star travel. Because by the time the Holbrooks neared Mars, Kern understood zero-point energy.

Each day their view of Mars grew bigger through the

Adventurer's port window. Dylan hung there, suspended, just watching. On the two hundred and first day of travel, when they finally approached the Mars docking port, it was Dylan whose voice shook with emotion. "We're here! We made it," he cried, as the Holbrooks put on spacesuits to step through the hatch onto an empty planet. Tears spilled from Dylan's eyes. Kern stayed dry-eyed.

The crew of four who'd been there for the previous sixteen months had already left, since arrivals and departures took place precisely when Earth and Mars reached the closest points in their orbits. Like Adam and Eve, Cain and Abel, the Holbrooks would have the planet all to themselves. But Mars — freezing, barren, and toxic — was no Paradise.

"Our new home!" Dylan exulted. Once inside the lava tube, where their living quarters were located, he went around with a wide grin on his face, touching the walls as though they were the walls of a cathedral. Kern hated it when Dylan grinned that goofy way. The gap between Dylan's front teeth had always bothered him, that space that had never been straightened because Dylan insisted, "What's it matter how I look? It won't change who I am."

On their first night on Mars, Kern announced, "I want the bottom bunk." Then he added politely, "If you don't mind, Dylan." The Evaluators were still tuned in to everything the Holbrooks said, though no longer with a video link. Just audio.

"Fine with me," Dylan answered. "Can you believe it's minus a hundred degrees outside? It's so warm in here."

"Thermal radiation from underground volcanic activity," their father said, coming in with the boys' spacesuits. He stood them in a corner; they were stiff enough to stay up by themselves. "Just hope the volcano doesn't decide to erupt while we're here."

"He's only joking," their mother countered, carrying in a gauge to measure the oxygen content of the room's air. "Everything's checking out just great. And you should see what the previous crew managed to grow in the greenhouse. Not just wheat and lettuce but peanuts and potatoes and tomatoes and strawberries. How'd you all like some reconstituted beef with real potatoes for dinner?"

"I'll help you, Mom," Dylan offered.

Although at first it felt weird to be pulled downward, once more, toward the center of a planet, soon enough they got used to Martian gravity, only three-eighths as strong as Earth's.

When they went outside for the first time, Dylan murmured, "I knew the sky was going to be pink instead of blue. I just didn't expect it to be so pretty." Raising his arms in his space suit, looking like a bulky ballerina, Dylan spun around and squeaked out the opening notes to the *New World* symphony. His voice — it was just starting to change — traveled electronically to the headset inside Kern's space helmet, making him grimace. Every sound the Holbrooks made not only crackled back and forth between the four of them but beamed back to Earth.

"Get serious, Dylan. The sky's pink because Martian dust in the atmosphere absorbs blue light. You know that." Kern didn't care about the sky, and he didn't especially care about the microbial life that might have existed, once, beneath the Martian surface. But he desperately wanted to be the first to find it.

His stay on Mars should be enough to put Kern at the top of the list of star-voyage candidates. But if he could dig up evidence of ancient life — well, that would give him the winning edge: He'd be chosen for sure. No one had yet discovered Martian life, not on the early robotic missions or on the later, manned missions.

Each of the four Holbrooks had a job to do. Janine, the boys' mom, converted elements on the Martian surface into oxygen, hydrogen, and methane to fuel their return trip, five hundred days in the future. And of course, they needed some of that oxygen for breathing.

Stewart, their dad, had to analyze Martian soil for signs of life, soil that Kern and Dylan dug up. That was the boys' job — the grunt work of digging and hauling dirt and rocks back to the lab. But the digging wasn't random; it was Kern who chose the exact spot for excavation each day.

Dylan daydreamed; Kern drudged. Mars might be where he was right then, but a star trip was what he hungered for. He worked so long every day that his father had to order him to quit, to come inside the crew quarters and breathe warm, oxygenated air, away from the frigid, thin, toxic, carbon-dioxide atmosphere, away from the harsh, cosmic-ray zapped, ultraviolet-bombarded, solar-flare fried surface of Mars.

Dylan seemed to enjoy all of it. Laughing, he said, "On Earth, I'm too young to drive a car. Here on Mars, I get to drive a $400 million dollar robotic rover all over the whole planet, with no cops to check my license. Va-room!" he yelled, doing wheelies in the red dust.

"Stop that!" Kern hissed. With his elbow, he poked Dylan in the ribs, which proved ineffective since the pressurized space suit cushioned the blow.

Each day, in the ten-mile-an-hour rover, the brothers ambled around boulders, searching out locations Kern had mapped the night before. They couldn't get lost because the area showed up in grids inside the visors of their space helmets. All they needed to do was follow the little green dot in front of their eyes; if the rover strayed, the dot turned red and the helmet beeped in warning.

They went where they were supposed to go, dug soil samples or picked up rocks precisely where the grid lines intersected, in the places Kern himself had picked out. After two hours — the longest it was safe to stay outside because of cosmic-ray bombardment — they drove back to crew quarters with a load of rock and soil. Robots could have done the job and could have stayed outside all the time, but humans did the job much better, much faster, and more accurately.

On each trip, each brother was supposed to gather ten samples and return them to their dad for preliminary analysis in the inflated fabric lab attached to their living quarters. Kern dug fast, labeled correctly, and always finished long before Dylan did.

"It's not that I'm slow, Kern," Dylan said. "It's that you're superfast." And he laughed, that tinny, amplified laugh that made Kern want to rip out both their headsets.

But Dylan *was* slow. He dug each sample with finicky attention, lifting it as carefully as if he were handling an embryo. He labeled it with a light touch, as though afraid the writing instrument might push too hard against the contents. When he finished each sample, he would hold it for a few extra minutes in his gloved hands, like a mother reluctant to say good-bye to a schoolchild.

After a month of this, Kern said, "It's okay, Dylan; I'll dig up more so you can look around, since you're so interested in the sky and soil and stuff." If Kern collected fifteen samples and Dylan slouched around gathering only five per day, that would triple Kern's chances of digging up something important.

"That's really nice of you, Kern, but I'd rather do it my way. You handle the samples too fast, too rough. If there's anything living in there, you could hurt it."

Anger throbbed in Kern's temples: His brother had just

criticized him in words that went out over an open audio connection to Earth. He wanted to yell at Dylan, but the Evaluators would be listening for Kern's reaction. Before he could sort out the best way to respond, Dylan went on, "You know, I've been thinking."

Lounging on a big red boulder, as much as it was possible to lounge wearing a bulky space suit, Dylan let his feet dangle and bent his head skyward. Bits of dry ice — the Martian equivalent of snow — drifted down to land and melt on the visor of his round helmet.

"You're always thinking when you're supposed to be working," Kern muttered, keeping his voice neutral, disguising the anger. "So what's it this time?"

"About how all this — " Dylan gestured at the Martian surface. "It's supposed to be terraformed in the next hundred years or so to make Mars Earthlike. Pumping even more carbon dioxide into the atmosphere to create a greenhouse effect. Warming the surface so liquid water can be stabilized."

None of this was new. It was Earth's long-range plan for the large-scale terraforming of Mars — changing it to be more like Earth so humans could colonize there. "So?" Kern grunted.

"Well, in my head, I have this picture. It's like I can see water from the poles and from under the surface piped into a whole city complex built under a clear dome. With lots of people. Hundreds! Not just four at a time. And then, all those people working to change the climate of

Mars, so eventually, maybe in two or three hundred more years, settlers can live outside the dome."

"Uh-huh. That's the plan." Kern began drilling through a rock so he wouldn't have to look at his brother.

"You know what, Kern? I hate that picture in my head."

"Huh?" Kern jerked upright. It sounded as though Dylan was about to say something negative concerning Earth policy. That could be a political mistake.

"I hate it, because — it would mean we're taking our own environment to another planet so *we* can survive. We might be able to terraform Mars over the next couple of centuries, but should we? We'd be destroying the Martian ecosystem to make way for our own. I don't think that's right."

Kern was on his feet now, shaking his head inside his helmet to signal Dylan to shut up. But Dylan didn't notice, or he pretended not to. Frantically, Kern waved his arms.

"Why are you pointing to your ear? Didn't you hear what I said? I said I don't think we ought to mess up Mars —"

Kern sank onto the seat of the rover. Back on Earth, all Dylan's words would be gone over, syllable by syllable. Would that ruin *Kern's* chances to be picked for interstellar travel — if his brother had radical thoughts? There was no way to turn him off: Dylan just kept talking.

" — because what if there really is life in these samples we're digging up, but we just don't know it when we see it?"

"You're wrong, Dylan," Kern interrupted loudly, choosing his words carefully for the benefit of the Evaluators listening in. "About terraforming Mars. We need the room. Earth's population is twelve billion now. Mars will give us a place to expand to, since it's the only other planet in the solar system humans can survive on. But we still need more room, so we've got to go outside our own solar system. To the stars."

Maybe Kern could turn his brother's disastrous statements around to make himself sound good. Confirming that he was speaking directly into the audio pickup inside his helmet, he added, "I'd give up everything, all the years of my life it would take to get there and back, if I could be the first person to find a new star with planets, where humans could survive. And build."

It was nearly impossible to read Dylan's expression behind the visor of the space helmet, but from the tilt of his head, he seemed to disapprove. "Kern," he said, "what if life is already there — on those unknown planets? Lots of mysterious combinations of atoms could create life that's a whole lot different from the life we know on Earth. What if we don't even recognize those life-forms, because they're so different? They could be trying to tell us that they're there, and we'd be too dense to pick up the message."

Growing emotional, Dylan jumped to his feet. "How would we know not to trample a different form of life, or starve it, or crowd it out? What if it's non-carbon-based life, and we don't even notice it? That's what I hate — us thinking we're so all-important we can move into space and take over."

"Now you're *really* wrong!" Dylan's wild rambling was turning Kern's anger into worry. "Listen!" he argued. "Nothing's more important than making sure human life survives — here on Mars, with terraforming, or out there, in the universe, with more terraforming. We need to fix up alien places so they'll support people. We have to!" I hope you'll put *that* in my record, Evaluators, he prayed under his breath.

And they did. Kern confirmed that they did, because each day he monitored NASA communications from Earth, including the confidential records kept there about the Holbrook family. Since he was a consummate hacker, he not only broke into his family's records, he also hacked every single audio mention of the starship now being constructed.

It already had a name. The *Valiant.* A spaceship built for one person only. Just one. Even with zero-point energy for propulsion, two people on board would require too much cargo. And on a twenty-year mission, each way, outside the solar system, there'd be no place to stop for supplies. Some would be stored at launch, but most of them would have to be grown onboard.

The next night, in their room inside the lava tube, Dylan sprawled on the floor, hugging a pillow to his chest, his eyes dreamy. As politely as he could, Kern asked, "Would you please move your legs so I can get in my bunk?" He said it nicely, but he'd much rather have stomped on his brother's shins to get his attention. What made Dylan think he could hog so much space in those cramped quarters?

"Oh, sorry," Dylan said, scrambling out of the way. "Sometimes I forget, Kern, about being considerate. But you — you're always considerate. You never forget."

You're right, I never forget, Kern thought. *Because the Evaluators never stop listening.*

"I think NASA was smart to try out a family unit like us," Dylan went on. "Four unrelated crew members can start irritating each other. Remember how we heard about that couple of guys on the first manned landing who got into a knock-down, drag-out fight? How they smashed up a water-filtration system? Fatally. It was fatal for the water system, I mean, not for the guys." Dylan laughed at his own dumb joke. "But us — we're used to each other's ways. We're family, so even if we do get irritated, we still love each other."

With a pillow around his ears, Kern blocked the sound of Dylan's easy, unamplified voice. It set Kern's teeth on edge.

The Martian days passed with a sameness that would have daunted anyone less ambitious then Kern or less easygoing than Dylan: a succession of pink skies, carbon-dioxide snowfalls, dust storms, and Martian sunsets, never seen with the unprotected eye but always through the tough aerogel visors of their helmets. And inside Kern's helmet, as unwelcome as static, the never-ending, laughing voice of his brother Dylan.

Then, after they'd spent three hundred eighty-nine of their scheduled five hundred days on Mars, Kern heard it. He'd hacked the audio file. It had been coded "Supremely Confidential," but that meant nothing, because Kern could crack any code. He told no one what he'd heard. He kept the news tightly coiled inside himself, like a snake dripping venom into his blood.

On day three hundred ninety, satellite tracking forecast a huge dust storm only hours away. Normally, Kern would have wanted to gather as many samples as possible before the family got stuck inside quarters for the duration of the storm. But this day, when he and Dylan reached the gridded area he'd chosen, Kern didn't start right in to dig. Why should he? Instead, he perched on a boulder, pressing the gloved index finger and middle finger of his right hand against his chest, hard.

"What are you doing?" Dylan asked.

Kern didn't answer. Only days before, he'd discovered how to apply a point of pressure to the single transistor that relayed his voice to Earth. If he pushed hard enough against the transistor, the signal to Earth would become garbled and stay that way for as long as twenty minutes — at best — making it impossible for the Evaluators to hear his voice. It was better than disconnecting the transistor altogether, which would alert Earth monitors that something had malfunctioned. This way, they'd blame the static on atmospheric disturbance. Twenty minutes, or even fifteen, ought to be enough for what Kern had to say to Dylan.

"Do exactly what I'm doing," he ordered Dylan. The other transistor, the one that connected the brothers' headsets, was unaffected, so they could hear each other perfectly. Their parents could hear them, too, if they wanted to, but their mother and father, busy with their own lab work, rarely bothered to make an audio check on the boys.

"Why should I do what you're doing?" Dylan asked.

"Just do it. Push hard, right against the first A in the NASA logo on your space suit. Yeah, like that. Hold it for about a minute. It screws up the signal, even after you quit pushing. You and I can hear each other, and Mom and Dad could hear us if they ever listened, but the Evaluators won't be able to get a fix on us because of the static. I don't want them to hear what we say."

Dylan answered with a chuckle, "Why? Gonna tell dirty jokes?"

"*You're* a joke," Kern spat. When he spoke the words, the rage rose up inside him like vomit, and this time he let it. "I was two years and two months old when you were born, and I remember every minute of our life right from the time you got there. You were a joke from the start. A bad joke. I hated it when you came."

Dylan said, "Yeah, I kind of figured that out, even way back then. If I picked up a toy, you grabbed it and kept it. Or hit me with it. Sibling rivalry, Mom used to say."

Kern growled, "You had no business getting born. We were a unit — Mom and Dad and I. I was the first son. The one with brains."

Raising his glove, Dylan rubbed dust from the visor of his helmet and peered toward the north, where the atmosphere had begun to thicken with dust. He said, "I don't like remembering when you were mean, Kern. Anyway, you stopped it soon enough."

"Yeah, I stopped it right when the Evaluators started monitoring us," Kern sneered. "Didn't you ever figure *that* out?"

After a moment, Dylan answered, "Let's get out of here. It looks like the storm's coming toward us pretty fast."

"You stay right there and listen to me!" Kern lashed out. His fists clenched as he remembered, "I was the first son, so Mom and Dad expected me to be perfect. I had to study all the time, but you — they let you get away with doing nothing. It made me crazy. I'd bust my brains studying calculus and quantum mechanics and astrophysics; you'd skim a book about butterflies or algae, and then you'd muck around in the dirt, looking for bugs and spores and stuff. And Mom and Dad thought that was just fine."

Dylan laughed. He was always laughing, it seemed, over the wrong things or over nothing. "They were waiting to see what direction I'd go. Anyway, I turned out okay. I aced all my exams at the academy, just like you did."

"That's why I got crazy — you never tried! Nobody pushed you; you just learned what you wanted to, and everybody said you were so great."

"Everybody but you, Kern."

Kern snarled, "On Earth, I could never show you how I really felt. The Evaluators were always spying on us to find out if we were 'a suitable family' to go to Mars. When I wanted to beat you bloody, I shoved it down inside me. When I wanted to tear your face off, I patted your grubby little head. 'Be nice to your brother, Kern,' Mom was always saying. So I pretended."

Slowly, Dylan raised himself to a stand. "I didn't know you were pretending. I thought you *were* nice." Not far from them, dust devils sucked up dancing red spirals from the planet's surface. Dylan's voice caught as he said, "I thought, because we were brothers, that you — you know — loved me."

"Well, I didn't. I hated you, but I hid it."

Dylan came closer. The visor of his helmet was only inches from Kern's. They stared at each other, although dust flaking around them made it hard to read each other's eyes. "And now?" Dylan asked, his voice low. "Do you still hate me?"

"More than ever." Kern stood up, getting a modicum of satisfaction from being four inches taller than his brother.

"Why? Why more than ever?"

"You don't care about the *Valiant*, you don't care about going to a star. I work, you slouch around, daydreaming. And get this! NASA picked you!"

"NASA — what?"

"They picked you!" Kern shrieked so loud inside his helmet that the sound, striking Dylan's headset, made him flinch. "You were chosen for the first voyage to a star."

Dylan seemed stunned. "Me? They picked me?"

"They say you're a nurturer. That you care about life — all the different life forms, recognizable or not. In the next ten years, they're saying, they'll train you to understand the chemistry of all known creation processes, and then — off you'll go. Alone, into the universe." Kern's laugh was mocking, bitter.

Softly, Dylan said, "You're angry about this."

"Oh, you noticed? You're right! *Because I wanted to go!*"

"Then go!" Dylan cried, shouting too. "I don't care!"

"What — I'm supposed to tell them my brother doesn't care, so choose me instead? As if they would!"

"Then both of us won't go," Dylan declared. "I don't want you to hate me."

"I can't help it!" This time it was Kern's voice that broke. He'd said it all, spewed out his hatred, but it didn't make him feel any better, especially when he saw Dylan's stricken expression. The visor couldn't hide Dylan's hurt.

Dust devils moved close now, too close, twisting like the demons that writhed in Kern. *Get a grip!* he told himself.

No matter how much tumult seethed inside him, he had duties to perform. He was responsible for himself and his brother. "Climb into the rover, Dylan," he ordered. "We have to go back while we can still see where we're driving."

"Not with you. Not with a brother who hates me. I'd rather walk." Instead of following Kern's command and turning toward the rover, Dylan took lumbering steps in the opposite direction.

"You can't walk, stupid. You'll get lost in the dust. Dylan, come back here! Dylan!"

Dylan kept going. It was hard to move with much speed in a spacesuit, but he managed to gain a substantial lead.

"Come here, idiot!" Kern yelled, but Dylan ignored him.

A new wave of anger tore through Kern. He clambered into the rover, revved it up, and pushed it faster than was safe, recklessly driving it straight at Dylan. At the last second he swerved the rover, barely missing his brother. Lunging out, he tackled Dylan just above his heavy boot tops. Both of them sprawled in the dust, Kern on top, twisting his brother's head as though he could wring Dylan's neck through the helmet's tough, transparent, unbreakable, molded aerogel.

Then he heard it, the hiss of escaping air. The impact had knocked a connecting bolt loose from the bottom of Dylan's helmet. Dylan tried to raise a hand to stop the leak, but Kern, using his knees, pinned Dylan's hands to the ground.

"Hey!"

"Yeah."

Both of them knew what it meant. When Dylan's space-suit lost enough pressure, his lungs would burst, his body fluids would boil, and he'd die quickly, in unbearable agony.

"You're faking it," Dylan said quietly. "You aren't really going to let it happen."

"I *am* letting it happen." An explosion of power surged through Kern, in his legs, in his arms, in his hands. He felt doubled in strength, as though his fury had made him invincible. He almost laughed as he forced Dylan's helmet hard against the dirt. The tiny stream of escaping air swirled a miniature cyclone of its own in the dust on the ground; Kern couldn't take his eyes off it. Making sure Dylan couldn't move, Kern fumbled to loosen the bolt that, with one more turn, would drop off and increase the tiny stream of pressurized air into a gusting jet, emptying Dylan's spacesuit.

"If you die," he muttered, "they'll call it an equipment failure. Their fault. So I'll tell them I want to take your place, to fulfill your destiny, Dylan. Then they'll have to let me go."

Dylan didn't even struggle. Fighting for breath, he said, "If you want it that much, go ahead and let me die."

Kern began to tremble so hard that the muscles of his arms shook in spasms as he held his brother down. Seconds passed, or were they full minutes? He tried to calculate how fast the air was escaping, but his mathematical genius had deserted him. As the air seeped out of Dylan's helmet, realization crept into Kern's soul — he was murdering his own brother! A heartbeat hammered in his ears — was it Dylan's? No, it had to be Kern's, because Dylan's heart was slowing, slowing, slowing to a stop, as the pressure fell low enough to collapse his blood vessels. Dylan's lips and eyelids were now blue, his face ashen. Soon blood would gush out of his mouth and his ears — would that happen just before or just after the actual moment of death? Maybe he was already dead.

"No! I don't want this!" With his right hand, Kern twisted the loose bolt back into place, fighting to tighten it, to block the air that kept up its ominous hiss as it bled out, lowering the pressure.

Suddenly their father's voice thundered into their headsets, "What's going on out there? Kern, where is your brother?"

"Why . . . are you asking me?" Kern stammered. "Am I in charge of Dylan?" Desperate, using all the strength in his awkward gloved fingers, Kern twisted the bolt one last quarter turn. Secure!

"Kern," their father's voice demanded again, "where is your brother?"

Dylan shuddered, barely moving. With enormous effort, gasping for air, he whispered, "I'm here, Dad."

Relief flooded Kern's head like the burst of a rocket. Dylan wasn't dead!

Their father said, "I had an alert from Earth that your communication was disrupted for a few minutes."

Only a few minutes! How many? How much had the Evaluators heard? Enough to know that Kern had tried to murder his brother? If they'd heard, Kern's future was destroyed, damaged beyond saving.

Still so weak he could barely whisper, Dylan said, "Dad, we were — goofing off. Wrestling. I started it. My fault."

Dylan was taking the blame! Stunned, Kern heaved himself to his feet as their father announced, "I'm signing off now. You boys come straight home, hear?"

Kern lifted his limp brother; as he did, he noticed the gouges left by their battle, deep scars dug into the red dust. No time to conceal the evidence — he half dragged, half carried Dylan to the rover, to the oxygen canister strapped there for that kind of emergency. "Breathe deep," he commanded after he hooked the tube to the narrow port on the side of Dylan's helmet. "Pull it in. You're gonna be okay."

Was it color coming back into Dylan's face or just the reflection of the Martian sky? Kern wasn't sure until Dylan gasped, coughing, "What about you, Kern? Are you going to be okay?"

"Me?" He didn't know — it depended on how much the Evaluators had heard. Nothing? Or everything! Maybe when the family returned to Earth, Kern would be charged with attempted murder, be deported to a prison colony far from his parents and his brother.

"Well, *are* you okay?" Dylan asked, obviously concerned.

For a long time Kern didn't answer. Dust blew around him, distorting his vision and his thoughts as if the gritty red particles were swirling through his brain. Then he said, "They were right all along, weren't they? When they picked you. You're the one who should go to a star. Not me."

The pain of it pierced Kern like a red-hot skewer, a pain that would never heal, yet he felt overpowering gratitude that his brother was alive. When he could control his voice, he said, "After we get back to Earth, I'm going to engineer design changes to the *Valiant* like no one's ever dreamed of. I've got so many great ideas, I'll get that ship to the stars in half the time." *If,* he said to himself, *I'm not sent into exile.*

There was no doubt that Kern could redesign the spaceship: He had supreme mathematical gifts, and he understood zero-point energy. Designing the *Valiant* would never be as good as flying it, but it was work he could willingly devote his life to, for his brother's sake and for the hope of his own redemption.

Even though the wind kept howling, there came a break in the storm, a sudden path of clear visibility. Dylan said, "We better get going while we can see."

As the rover headed toward home base, wind blew dust into the Martian sky, erasing telltale signs of deadly conflict. But the storm was far from over. Martian storms came and went. This one would end. Another would follow.

They were part of the planet.

Author's Note

In the summer of 1997, I sat spellbound watching a small robotic rover named Sojourner *creep across the surface of Mars, sending us close-up, televised pictures of a world we'd never before seen. I learned about NASA's plans to deliver the first humans to Mars by — the date ranges anywhere from 2011 to 2030, depending on a lot of variables, including luck.*

But what about a human family *on Mars? I wondered. Two parents, two children, confined to an alien planet with no other people on it — would they be like Adam and Eve, Cain and Abel, all alone on Earth? Would there be the same rivalry between the brothers, a rivalry that turned murderous? Using real science facts about the present and future of the inhospitable red planet, I wrote "His Brother's Keeper."*

A ROBOT DOESN'T HAVE A CURVE BALL

Ron Koertge

I squatted behind the plate, pulled down my face mask, and got ready for the first pitch of the millennium.

Sixty feet and six inches away, Dan blew on his fingers, then reached into his glove. He eyed me, shook off my first sign, nodded at the second.

"Take it easy," I yelled. "It's a long season."

His tight jaw didn't even twitch. He was practicing his game face. First time he'd had it on since summer league. He stretched and let it fly.

I had to reach. "What kind of slider was that? Try a curve this time."

"That was a curve." He rotated one arm, like a little kid playing windmill. "I'm stiff, man."

"I told you we should've played more catch." I faked a big overhand toss but didn't let go because it was great to feel the ball again, the code of the stitches in my hand. Great to feel my body move in ways it hadn't all winter.

Danny lobbed a few; then he turned on the heat. My left hand, buried in the mitt, started to sting a little.

I pressed on the air like catchers do, motioning for him to take it easy. I walked toward him maybe ten feet or so.

"You going to the dance?" I asked.

He was bringing up his knee, watching it descend. Working on his mechanics. "What dance?"

"The Spring Fling. Or at least that's what the banner across the front of the art building said."

"Oh, yeah." Dan frowned and stepped off the mound. "Are you going?"

"Everybody's going."

"So who'd you ask?"

"Nobody. How about you?"

"I asked Nobody, too. She said she was going with you."

That made me smile. Dan could almost always make me feel better, which is good. Because I'm a little miserable most of the time. Most kids are. Most *people* are. Especially since this is the year 2000 and nothing's changed. It's in all the papers and on TV; everybody thought it'd make such a difference, getting away from all those nasty nineteen hundreds and into the terrific twos. And what really happened? Nada. Nothing. Zero. Zilch. Squat. Our folks go to work; we go to school.

At least we've got baseball.

He threw one sidearm, then flexed his wrist, checking for motion. I lobbed it back.

"We could go to the dance stag," I said.

"If we go together, we wouldn't be stag, would we?"

"We'd be two stags."

"Can stags do that, Lee?"

"If they don't rub each other's antlers."

"It's been a long winter, my friend. It's time you got out of the house."

My legs were starting to ache, so I stood up. "Let's say I ask somebody. My parents drive over to her house, I trudge up the walk and face her father; then my folks drop us off at the dance, pick us up again three hours later, and wait in the car while I walk her to the door. That sucks so intensely. In sixteen months I get my license. I'll start dancing then."

"Ethan asked Ann, and he said they're just going to meet there."

"Big Ann or Little Ann?"

"Big Ann. Why? Are you thinking about Little Ann?"

"No way. When you dance, her nose is like in your belly button."

"And that's a bad thing?" He stepped all the way off the mound. "So who?" he asked.

"Leslie."

"Yeah! Leslie is fresh!"

I covered my ears like he'd dropped a cherry bomb into the nearest trash can. "Do you think they heard you in Montana?"

"What's the problem? She likes you. Toby told me."

"Oh, great. Let's believe Toby, whose father said the world was going to end last year."

"Millennium fever. A lot of people had that."

"A lot of people didn't stop doing their homework like Toby."

"Speaking of homework," Dan interrupted, "don't look now; here comes Walter."

"In his blue Doc Martens."

"They match his hair."

"It's kind of cool he did that," I said. "Most science geeks don't bother."

"Most science geeks don't play second base, either."

Walter found a fairly dry spot on the brown grass and stacked his textbooks like he was building a pyramid to Ra. He watched Dan throw some smoke.

"You guys are gonna go all the way to the majors together," he yelled. "You'll be the next great black-and-white battery."

"Dan is black?" I frowned and turned to my buddy. "You never told me you were black."

"Hey, you never asked."

"Very funny," said Walter taking a cling-wrapped sandwich out of his book bag.

We watched him eat. He took precise bites and chewed each one a long time. "Are you going to finish that in time for the dance?" I asked.

He took a swig of bottled water. "Dances are a waste of time."

"Which means," Dan said, "that he asked and got shot down."

"You don't get into Cal Tech going to dances, guys."

"That's where you're wrong, Walter," I said. "You have to rumba to get into Cal Tech. Everybody knows that."

"So who wouldn't go to the dance with you?" asked Dan. "Or is the list so long that we'll be late for dinner."

Walter tucked his long hair behind both ears, which seemed to have been created for exactly that. He lowered his head.

"It was so bad," he muttered. "I'm still, like, totally sick at my stomach. First of all, I had to wait about twenty years until she was alone."

Danny walked all the way to the baseline where Walter sat. He put a consoling hand on one thin shoulder. "You have to have that wolf mentality, buddy. Trail them until the weakest drops back; then you swoop down, cut her out of the herd, and ask her for a date."

"Actually, that's what I did. I followed them until Ann stopped to look in a store window."

"You asked Little Ann?"

"Who else, Lee? *I'm* little."

I looked at Walter. "You're little? You never told me you were little."

Dan scooted closer. "Just ignore him. I'm listening. You get her alone at the window, you ask her, and — ?"

"Okay. So I do that. I get her alone. My heart's pounding, my palms are sweaty. I stutter. But I ask her." Walter dropped his head into both palms. "Oh, God."

"I take it she didn't say yes."

"She didn't say anything."

I nudged my mask higher on my forehead. "So what happened? She's not still standing there, is she?"

Walter sighed. "After about an hour, she yelled, 'Wait for me!' and ran up the block."

Dan rubbed a little dirt into the baseball. "In second grade when they ran away, it meant they liked you."

"But this is tenth grade," I told him, "and there's plenty of fish in the sea."

"Not short fish. And not as cute." Walter got to his feet. He clenched his fists. "This dating crap is so frustrating. Five years from now, ten tops, it'll be way better."

I cocked my head. "Why's that?"

"For one thing, absolutely everybody'll be online."

Dan shrugged. "So?"

"So we'll all be in the privacy of our own homes," Walter said. "Nobody'll be nervous."

I planted both feet and held out my arms like I was angling down the face of a wave. "You're not nervous when you surf the old net?"

Walter shook his head. "Nope. For one thing, I'm not short."

"Excuse me?"

"I mean nobody knows I'm short, so I don't think about it."

Dan leaned forward. "What do you say when somebody asks how tall you are?"

"They don't ask stuff like that."

"Pretty bogus chat room." Dan knocked some dirt out of his cleats.

"Well, okay. Sometimes. Like on weekends."

I nodded. "When the question of height often rears its ugly head."

"So," Dan asked, "what do you tell 'em on weekends, Walter?"

"The truth, okay? I tell 'em the truth. But it's, like, it doesn't matter so much because nobody can see me. In hyperspace, short is a relative term."

I told him that he was a braver man than I. "I'd lie about these zits."

"Well, pretty soon you won't be able to lie, 'cause you'll be sitting at your computer and there'll be, like, this red light that flashes if you do."

Dan scowled. "I don't even want to hear this, Walter."

"Well, it's coming. I saw a picture of it. You still use your mouse, okay? But there's this thing on it that's really a miniature polygraph."

I held up my mitt like I was checking for rain, leaned forward, and let my mask tumble into it. "So it's Saturday night on Earth," I mused, "sometime in the future, and these super-unstressed people are sitting around with their fingers in these teensy-weensy lie detectors, and that's dating?"

"Right."

"But what do you do besides sit there?" asked Dan.

"Pretty much anything you do on a real date: watch the same movie, eat popcorn —"

"You're in different parts of the city eating popcorn?"

"But you can, like, hear the other person chew and stuff 'cause you're both wearing these like very high-tech, super-sensitive body suits," said Walter. "So you're virtually together."

"But not really," I said.

He held his thumb and forefinger a micromillimeter apart. "Very, very, very close."

I leaned toward him. "But not really."

"You can hardly tell the difference."

I leaned closer. "But there is a difference."

"Virtually none."

Dan pushed me out of the way. "Why don't people just listen to each other chew in a real movie?"

"'Cause virtual is better."

"Virtual kissing is better than real kissing? Are you nuts? Technology is never gonna be that good."

"Well, for sure it's safer: no mono, no bad breath . . . "

I took hold of his shirt and shook him a couple of times. "But, Walter, you hypertool, there's no breath at all!"

"Okay, forget kissing. Say Dan blows out a rotator cuff Wednesday. Dr. Cyborg just makes him a new one, and he pitches again Thursday."

Dan frowned. "How'd I blow out a rotator cuff? I thought I was wearing my super-sensitive, high-tech body suit with one finger stuck in the lie detecting mouse."

"You'd find a way, ace. Or let's say you need some major organ; you just replace it. Everybody'll live forever."

"Sounds like long lines at the ATM," I said.

"Money will be in museums. Curiosity pieces. There'll just be debit chips. Everything'll be different."

"Well, not baseball. No way am I giving up baseball."

Walter shook his head. "You don't have to give it up, Dan. Just plug in a sports module."

"And then what? Have virtual Mom wash the virtual grass stains out of my virtual uniform? No way."

"Well, at least there won't be any more of that racial stuff."

"And why's that?"

Walter looked smug. "No races. No black people. Or yellow people or white people. We'll all be the same."

"Hey, I like being black."

"You can always jack into the black experience."

Dan looked suspicious. "I know I shouldn't ask this, but what color are we all going to be?"

"Beige."

Dan and I just about collapsed. We fell all over each other. A couple of kids walking home on the third base side stared at us, we were laughing so hard.

When I was pulled together again, I said, "My grandma told me that when she was our age, like back in the fifties, everybody was sure that by 2000 we'd all be wearing silver jumpsuits and zipping around in hovermobiles."

Dan tugged at his Cardinals cap. "And what'd we get instead? Extra wide, extra baggy jeans from the Gap and the new VW Beetle, which looks a whole lot like the old VW Beetle."

Walter leaned in. "But other stuff changed. Lee's grandma had never heard of computers, and now they're everywhere. And she couldn't have been friends with your grandma, Danny, because races were, like, almost totally separate back then."

Dan looked unimpressed. "Yeah, but we also got AIDS and a rain forest about as big as a patio." He tossed the ball into the air and caught it behind his back. "Man, remember midnight 1999? That was supposed to be such a big deal. And what really happened? A million people got drunk and puked, that's what happened."

"Not all at once," I pointed out. "They puked according to their time zones, moving from east to west."

"Whatever. So where were your robots with their mops and aspirins then?"

"They'll happen." Walter was decisive. "They're being built. And I sure wish I'd had one yesterday. I would've had it go meet Ann's robot, and I would've just stayed home and not got dumped on."

"Because you would've wisely programmed it to break it to you gently?" I asked.

"Anyway," Dan pointed out, "she didn't say no. She didn't say anything. What's your robot going to do with that?"

Walter acted patient. "You're thinking of replicants, Lee. Robots just do whatever you tell them to."

"My grandma's really funny about robots," I said. "They *were* the year 2000 to her. She's totally steamed she hasn't got one. She was supposed to be able to sit around and these cute little aluminum guys would clean the toilet and vacuum and stuff. So now every time Grand-dad doesn't take out the garbage, she yells, 'Where's the robot?'"

"There'll probably be robot baseball," said Walter. "We'll watch it from the safety of our cocoons."

Only about three feet separated them, but Danny charged like he'd been brushed back hard. "There's not going to be any robot baseball! Robots don't have curve balls."

"Hey, you can build a robot that'd throw the wickedest —"

"No, no. Every curve is different." He appealed to me. "Right, Lee?"

I stepped up beside him. "Right."

"Guys, you program in the differences."

Dan shoved him. "Shut up, Walter!"

Walter shoved back. "Hey, I know what I know."

That's when I spotted the girls. "Break it up, you guys. There's Ann and Leslie."

"And," said Dan, "Heather Nyguen. Too bad she's going with Rasheed."

"They broke up," Walter informed us.

I asked where he got that scoop. "One of your chat rooms?"

"Toby told me."

"Man, Toby didn't used to know anything. Toby was totally out of it. How come all of a sudden Toby knows everything?"

Walter looked smug. "He's online, Lee. He's plugged in. So is Leslie, e-mail address and everything."

"Hey, if I want to talk to Leslie I'll call her on the phone. If I want to read on a screen, I'll go to a foreign film."

Then Dan leaned toward Walter. "You know, future boy, Little Ann is checking you out." He grabbed Walter's arm and hissed. "Don't look! Did you forget the rules, man? She looks at you, I see her doing it and tell you. Then you look at me; she sees that and knows that you know. If you want to look, look at Leslie, who should be looking at Lee."

"I just got an idea," said Walter.

"Put your hands around it and blow gently, or it'll go out."

"Let's all three of us go over there and talk to all three of them. If you guys asked Leslie and Heather to the dance, Ann'd probably say yes, too."

"Walter, buddy, I don't know. You've about got me convinced dating is a hassle. I might just stay home and download a few slow dances. How about you, Danny?"

"Sounds good. I could dance with myself, then —"

"They're leaving!" Walter sat up straight.

"No, it's okay." Dan pointed. "They just migrated a few yards."

"You know," I said, "I saw this show on the Animal Channel where these little clusters of beasties do all this mysterioso preening and pawing the ground and —"

"Then," Dan said, "you and I have to butt heads, and the winner leads all three of those babes into a beautiful meadow with a brook."

"Either that or I've got brighter feathers and they choose me while you go up on Echo Mountain and cry."

Walter grabbed one of his books, opened it, and leaned into it studiously. "What are they doing now?" he hissed.

"They're wondering," Dan said, "if you're a real dork or a virtual dork."

Walter slammed the book shut. "God, I hate this. By 2050, we'll have these computer-generated ideal partners. Just type in what you want, and there she is."

"Is this like driving up to the clown," I asked, "and ordering two burgers and a malt?"

Walter wouldn't laugh. "You guys like baseball so much? Order a couple of girls who know every statistic since Abner Doubleday."

Dan put his mitt on his head like a hat. "Can you imagine how boring that would be?"

"Yeah, Walter. They'd know stuff, but it wouldn't mean anything to them."

"So?"

Dan retrieved his glove and pounded one fist into it. "Are you nuts, man? You seriously think it'd be fun to talk to some robo-babe who knew everything about a game she'd never played?"

I stepped between them. "Guys, while we debate the issue of virtual girls, some real ones are standing right over there wondering what's taking us so long."

Dan pointed Walter in the right direction. "C'mon, wirehead. We're going to stroll over there and ask them what's up. They're going to say they're on their way to Victoria's Secret and do we want to come along. Then we're going to say that we'll think about it."

Walter turned to me. "I'm serious, Lee."

"Okay. We're seriously going to go over there, say hi, and talk about how stupid school is."

Walter felt his stomach. "I'm so nervous. Who's gonna bring up the dance?"

"I'll take care of that," I said.

Walter brightened. "Maybe we should all ask at the same time?"

"What are we, the glee club?"

"You know," said Dan, "he's right for once. It doesn't have to be boy-girl, boy-girl, boy-girl. We can just go. All six of us. My grandma'll drive."

"Your grandma is so cool. Remember when she took us to get our ears pierced?"

"And Mom grounded *her* for a week?"

I nodded. "If I was going to order a grandma, I'd want one just like her. But I wouldn't know what to ask for, you know? She's, like, unique."

"Pretty soon," said Walter, "we can clone her. Then everybody'd have a cool grandma."

I glowered at him. "But she wouldn't be cool then, doofus. She's cool because there's just one of her."

Dan shoved him playfully. "Like there's just one of you, Walter. Which is one too many."

"Man, if I could, I'd just order a new everything." He looked down at his thin chest. "This skinny body is one major burden."

"You think Little Ann would like this brand-new, tall, totally buff Walter?"

"Are you kidding? Absolutely."

"You'd scare her, man. Ann's shy," I reminded him.

"Everybody knows that. She likes you 'cause you're shy, too."

"If she likes me so much, why didn't she say anything when I asked her to the dance?" Walter groaned. "God, I hate this. Twenty years from now —"

I held up one hand, like a traffic cop. "Stop with the future, okay? The dance is Saturday."

Walter sagged. "I know, I know."

I got my friends on their feet. "C'mon."

"So we're not asking individuals, right? It's for sure let's-all-go-together?"

Dan nodded. "Trust the Animal Channel, Walter. Things'll naturally sort themselves out later on."

"Yeah," I said. "So just pretend you're grazing and nibble your way over there."

"I should have e-mailed her."

Dan shook his head. "Too late now."

We all took a deep breath and headed for Leslie, Ann, and Heather.

When we got there, when we were actually facing the three girls, Walter just froze. Even Dan lost his nerve and could only stare at Heather.

So it was up to me. I looked through my personal thesaurus for just the right thing to say, the perfect word that would break the ice and win their hearts, too.

"Hi," I said.

Leslie looked up, looked right at me, and smiled. "Hi."

"We were just thinking," I said, "about the dance. And we were wondering if you guys wanted to go, you know? With us. Danny's grandma's got a van. She'd drive and phone all your folks if you want."

Heather nodded and Ann blushed.

Leslie smiled and said, "Great."

"All right! I'll call you," I said, "later."

"E-mail me," she replied, "lesliecool dot com."

Then they bolted.

Walter looked at me. "Is that it? They're gonna go?"

"Of course, they're gonna go," I said. "Let me tell you a story, okay? About a million years ago some nervous guys with clubs in one hand and wrist corsages in the other were going from cave to cave looking for dates for the rock concert, and I'm talking real rocks."

Dan grinned and held out his fist for me to tap.

"Well, we're part of that story, man. Some piece of DNA from back then is still tucked into us somewhere 'cause we're human, not some virtual hunk of virtual junk that just does what somebody tells it to."

"Whatever. I'm just glad it's over." Walter checked his watch. "I gotta go."

We watched him trudge off the field. Then Dan turned on his heel and trotted halfway to the mound. He stood there, rotating the ball in his palm. I stepped behind the plate.

All of a sudden, Danny stalked back to me. "There's not

gonna be robot baseball, is there? 'Cause I'm not givin' this up." He pointed. "Most of the things I know I learned between here and home plate."

"Relax. There's two things that are never gonna change. There's always gonna be a spring dance, and guys are always gonna play ball."

"You're sure?"

"Absolutely."

"Even if there are robots, we'll come out anyway, okay?"

"We'll kick their aluminum butts."

"Good." He ground the rubber with his cleats. "That Walter, man. He gets on my nerves."

"Forget him. It's spring of the year 2000. You've got a great curve ball, a decent slider, and a baffling change. *And* a date for the dance." I squatted down. "So burn one in here. Show me what you've got."

Author's Note

I was born in 1940, and many people of my generation were promised a life of relative ease. The word "automation" was tossed around a lot, and any artist's rendering of the future always showed monorails, glass-domed cities, and people in one-piece jumpsuits.

Part of this easy life was going to be due to robots. They'd do the housework, cook, and pack lunches. They'd mind the baby, wash the sky-mobile, and remind us of our rare doctor's appointments, where we'd have a faulty organ replaced and then be home in time for dinner, a dinner prepared, of course, by one or more of our trusty, selfless, metallic friends.

Of course, it didn't happen. But it doesn't take a writer long to start wondering "what if?" Tinkering with an American staple like base-

ball appealed to me. So I played the "what if?" game and decided to suggest that not only baseball but an even more American staple — dating — could only be impoverished by high-tech gadgetry of all kinds.

RAGE

Lois Lowry

op was born in 1900 and had always said that he would live to see the year 2000. He planned to die quietly after the world had moved into a new century.

He was my great-grandfather.

"Yessir, BJ," he used to tell me, "right here in my bed, with a smile on my face. You'll be the one to find me. You tuck me in good if I need it. You straighten things up. Square off the corners of that there rug. It always goes askew. And then call your mom. She'll take care of the rest."

"Do not go gentle into that good night," a poet said. We read the poem in my college prep English class and it made me think of Pop. Pop was going to go gentle if I had anything to do with it. I took him his coffee every morning. A little milk, no sugar, good and hot: That was how he liked it. He puttered all day, on his own, while I was at school; but at night I tucked him in, and I always left him smiling, even if his day had gone badly. I had a whole storehouse of stupid jokes that still coaxed a grin from him, even the ones he'd heard often before.

"It's the way you tell it, BJ," he would say. "You got a gift." And he would chuckle his way out of whatever had gotten him down in the dumps.

He made it. He made it to the millennium. He would have turned one hundred a couple of months later, but he left with the century instead. He did not go gentle. He went out with his deer rifle blazing, two dogs dead, and three people wounded. He would have been hauled off to jail and become the oldest prisoner on record if he hadn't had a heart attack with his finger still on the trigger of the gun.

He had outlived his wife by thirty years, and most of his children were dead. "War and pestilence," he used to say, because five of the seven had died either in combat or of cancer. And his grandchildren, too: My father, killed in a car accident when I was nine, was one of twenty grandchildren; and many, like my dad, were gone. Most of them car wrecks. Two drug overdoses and a suicide, though maybe those are both the same thing if you consider it.

I was one of countless great-grandchildren. But I was the one who had his name and lived nearby. From the time I was twelve and Pop was ninety-four, I went to the farm each evening, kept him company, told him jokes, and slept there in the spare room so that he wouldn't be alone.

We still called it the farm, though it wasn't anymore.

"Right in that room, BJ," he told me often. "That's where I was born, in that room where you sleep. In that same bed. People didn't go to hospitals then, the way they do now."

"Your mother probably got up and milked the cows that evening," I told him once, with a grin. We were eating supper together at the old kitchen table. I cooked for him, mostly. Simple stuff. Canned soup and hamburgers. Or my mom brought casseroles over.

He punched my shoulder, chuckling, appreciating the joke. "Probably plowed a few acres the next day," he said. But then, his expression darkened, and he glanced through the window. It must have been summer, then. It was still light at suppertime, the sun slipping down toward the horizon, sky bleeding into the hills. The kitchen windows faced south, and there were still fields there, still a few sagging fences. There had been no animals in those pastures for years, but the wooden fence boards, faded and cracking, still cut a pattern across the land.

"Few acres," he repeated bitterly, the joke of it gone. Anger colored the map of his face. His skin was mottled

and papery thin, and you could see the veins mapped behind it; a place on his forehead throbbed, and even the
brittle threads of his eyebrows seemed to vibrate with his
sudden but predictable fury.

"I'll pour you some coffee, Pop," I said quickly, dis-
tracting him. It was a mistake, always, to mention the
early days of the farm, the expanse of its acreage. But there
were so few things left to talk about with him. He had no
interest anymore in the day-to-day gossip of our tiny
town: the school board arguments, the budget for snow
removal, the scandalous divorce of the dentist and his
sullen, big-haired wife. A shopping mall was being built
down the highway, and the business owners on Main
Street — all fourteen of them — felt threatened. Pop
didn't care. Pop hadn't visited Main Street in years except
for an occasional trip to the barber or the doctor, both of
them strangers to him, too young, in Pop's opinion, to
know their trades.

In 1998 I got my license. I was sixteen. Pop went with
me for my first legal drive. He watched, swiveling his neck
from the passenger seat, while I backed his old Chevy out
of the barn where it had been stored since he quit driving,
reluctantly, at ninety, eight years before. My parents had
tended it for him, first my dad and then my mom keeping
it up after my dad died, keeping its registration and insur-
ance up, driving it occasionally so that it wouldn't simply
dry up and die. She had done it for me, knowing the car
would be mine when I was old enough; and for herself, so

that eventually she could turn the errands over to me and gain back a little life of her own. And it was for Pop, too; the car was part of him, the engine with its smooth surge of power like his heart, its dents and chips like his own healed wounds.

"Turn right," he directed me when I edged it out to the road at the end of the barn driveway that first time, two years ago. So I did, and we cruised slowly in toward town, passing the official sign: WELCOME TO COLLYERVILLE, settled 1752. Population 863. We drove past the shuttered houses and unpainted barns that had stood sentinel along this road for centuries, past their rutted driveways, weathered fences, and tilted mailbox posts.

"Look. Someone bought the Woodman place," I told Pop, and slowed the car as we went by the house, scaffolding against its side, one wall glistening with new white paint, the rest waiting. Peeling shutters were stacked on the ground, and there was an extension ladder propped by the porch. He stared. He wasn't looking at the house so much as the surrounding land.

"Pasture's the same," he said. "Nobody's going to build on that pasture, are they?"

I didn't know, but pretended I did, to reassure him. "I think they're probably going to have horses there, Pop," I said.

He blew out a half whistle of relief. "That's good," he said. "Yeah, that's good, BJ. Horses. That pasture always had horses."

We cruised down Main Street. I was hoping to see friends — this was my first time driving in public; there was a girl named Sandra I was hoping to impress — but it was a Saturday morning and no one much around.

"What's at the pictures?" Pop asked.

I glanced over at the marquee of the town theater, but the letters, one missing, spelled CL SED. "The theater's closed down, Pop," I told him. "There's a new complex at the mall: six different theaters. I could take you there sometime, now I have my license."

He snorted in disgust. At the other end of town I pulled into a Dairy Queen and bought him a vanilla cone. "Have a nice day," the girl behind the window said when she handed it to me. I recognized her as a girl who had graduated a couple of years before. I think she had married a guy from her class.

"Ready to head home?" I asked him as I pulled away from the Dairy Queen. I clicked on the right blinker, intending to turn down the back road that would circle the south side of town and bring us around again to the farm.

"Not that way," he said fiercely. I saw from the corner of my eye how his hands tightened, how his fingers dug into the cotton trousers across the knobs of his knees.

So I eased off on the accelerator, pulled into a driveway, and turned the car around. I headed back down Main Street, the way we had come. The theater was showing CLOS D from this side.

I'd been testing him, I guess. Stupid. I knew he could not approach the farm from the west. My mother, driving him on his errands, had become accustomed to the circuitous routes she had to take. But I was impatient with it. "What's the big deal?" I had asked her once. "It's not going to kill him to — "

"It could, BJ," she said with a sympathetic shrug. "I know it seems crazy. But it makes him so angry. I really think that kind of anger could maybe kill him."

Watching him that day, that quick moment when his hands dug at his own knees, I thought she was right. He was so old — and so small, his legs like twigs in baggy khakis, his torso just a stem wrapped badly in a faded, too-big flannel shirt — but in that moment I saw the immensity of his wrath.

So I drove him home from the east. LEAVING COLLY-ERVILLE. Coming over the rise that brought the little farmhouse into view, another sign, official, white-on-green state lettering, was posted on the shoulder of the road. STATE PRISON. WARNING. DO NOT PICK UP HITCHHIKERS.

He turned his eyes to the barn, to the passage that connected it to the kitchen, to the familiarity of the little porch with its pillowed wicker chairs and the flowerpot heavy with pink geraniums. He had learned to blind himself to the prison. The ominous structures, looming brick buildings surrounded by impenetrable fencing, lay immediately beyond the farm. Late in the day, as the sun lowered, the prison shadows moved over Pop's small yard and crept up the west side of his house. The window shades on that side were always drawn.

He had sold the land in 1976. He was widowed by then, and his children, those still living, were grown and gone. But the war in Vietnam had wound to a halt at last, and Pop hoped that a grandson or two would come home to Collyerville, would settle in with him and help him farm. It just didn't happen. My own father had been a biology teacher at the regional high school; I saw his name every day, walking through the hall where the science classes were. A lab was named in his honor; there was a small bronze plaque. He was thirty-nine when the late-day sun blinded him at an ungated train crossing.

"You should have been here back then, BJ," Pop always told me. "You were born too late. I would have put you on the deed. You got my name, and you should have got my farm."

It did no harm for me to lie to him and pretend I would've wanted it.

"This land was alive, BJ," he said. "You could hear it singing. Lord, on a summer evening I'd stand out there by that shed, and it was so loud I'd almost have to clap my hands over my ears. The cows and the birds and the insects. The breeze rattling the leaves on that big maple tree. There was an elm back then, too. It stood over to the west — "

He gestured to the darkened windows on the west side of

the house. "It was the first thing they took down. They said it was diseased." His voice took on the familiar bitterness.

"There was a lot of elm blight, Pop. The trees on Main Street all had to come down, too."

But facts were no solace to him. He sold the land, and his two-hundred-year-old elm tree with it, because he couldn't farm it anymore, and he sold it in good faith to state officials who talked about a nature sanctuary. They paid him an amount of money that allowed him to live his remaining days in comfort and security, and he planned to spend those days listening to the birds in the evening and watching the western hills as the sun slipped behind them.

But the sanctuary they had planned for Pop's acreage to the west was for a kind of nature that had begun to evolve in our state and every other. They had needed an isolated site for the increasing criminal population. The state had outgrown its prisons. A year after the contract for the sale was signed, the huge hole from the uprooted elm still raw, they came with surveyors and architects. Pop watched them measure out the perimeter that would become fence, dotted with watchtowers; then the parallel perimeter that would become inner fence, and finally the rectangles that would eventually become home, future, deathbed, and coffin to violent men with vacant, hardened eyes.

For me, it had always been there. I knew no other landscape. And I learned early to pretend in Pop's presence that it didn't exist.

But when I was young, it fascinated me. We visited Pop

each Saturday and helped him with small household chores. Assigned to keep an eye on my baby sister as she played in the yard, I stood on the farmhouse porch, looking up at the watchtowers, seeing the outlined heads of guards, imagining their high-powered guns. I fantasized escapes: tunnels dug with sharpened spoons under the yard, crazed criminals emerging dirt-smeared near the peonies, entering the farmhouse at night, cutting the phone lines, stealing Pop's deer-hunting rifle from its locked cabinet, making their way to freedom, maybe on a Mexico beach, driving the old Chevy across the border after a high-speed chase through the Midwest and down across Texas. I knew my maps; there was one on my lunchbox. And I watched too much TV.

Nine or ten years old, mourning my father but bored by grief, I pulled the parlor shade aside while Mom, my little sister in her lap, sat with Pop in the kitchen sipping coffee. I watched weekend visitors drive into the parking lot across the road. Gun molls, I thought theatrically, staring at women who checked their bright lipstick in tilted rearview mirrors before emerging from their cars. She drove the getaway car, but he didn't rat on her. I wondered if any of them could smuggle in a weapon.

Stealthily I made twin pistols out of my extended index fingers and shot these women, picking them off one by one as they crossed the road. With satisfaction I imagined their astonished expressions when they realized I had recognized their guilt and leveled them with well-aimed single bullets into the heart. I left them sprawled on the shoulder of the road: piles of them, heaps of moll bodies, and slipped the shade back when Mom called me out of the darkened parlor of daydreams to come to the kitchen for lunch.

By the time I turned twelve and Pop needed me at night, I had lost interest in the imagined underworld of horror next door. I biked to the farm every afternoon and began to sleep in the spare bedroom without a wasted moment of fear that peonies would topple to reveal tunneling killers in the night. By twelve I was addicted to video games, fantasies of girls who would be willing to kiss me (none ever had), and a complex, ongoing daydream starring BJ the Bondlike, who drove a sleek sports car and talked with a sneer.

I began to notice, spending nights at Pop's, the noise from the west. During the day it seemed to blend with other, more official, more routine sounds: slammed doors, a loud whistle announcing noon each day, a loudspeaker with unintelligible announcements. But at night the other noise began. Banging percussion: rhythmic, metal on metal. Raucous shouts. I could hear men's hard laughter, sometimes; and an occasional solo obscenity hurled out, echoed by others, mocking and muffled. Occasionally the noise would rise until I could almost picture some kind of operatic performance taking place behind the walls: a huge stage of baritones hurling shouted discord into the air while an accompanying orchestra frantically clanked and banged on steel pipes. Then it would subside, cut off by a staccato order from the loudspeaker.

I was surprised that you couldn't hear the dogs. At night they released trained Dobermans who prowled and guarded the perimeter between the two fences. Most dogs I knew had easy, boisterous barks: pleased woofs of greeting or agitated yips of discomfort. But the Dobermans were silent. I watched them move through the shadows, muscles taut and eyes alert. But they made no sound.

The girl named Sandra noticed me eventually. She wasn't my future, I knew, but she was a pretty good here-and-now. She had a sure, self-confident way of talking that I liked and a way of tossing her short dark hair back that looked like a gesture of invitation. Her dad was a real estate agent; her family lived on one of the side streets in town in a house painted deep gold, with black shutters. She said they moved from house to house. When an offer was high enough, they simply sold where they lived, packed up, and went to some other unsold dwelling, and her mother started stitching draperies and painting woodwork again.

"All it takes is the right wallpaper," Sandra said. "Maybe some tile work. And sometimes, new windows. Buyers always look at windows. They try them. If a window sticks, sometimes a sale falls through. So we get rid of old windows or fix them up with new sash weights, and we strip the peeling paint and reglaze the panes.

"Then next thing you know, someone comes along and says, 'I'll take it,' and we start packing again."

It seemed an odd, gypsylike way of life to me, since my own was burdened so little by transition. But I was fascinated by her flippant, agreeable approach to change. Pop liked her, too. She came often to the farmhouse in the evening, and we did our homework together in his kitchen while he dozed in his chair, CNN proceeding unwatched on the screen.

"Wolf Blitzer." Pop sat up suddenly one evening, as if he'd been startled awake. He stared at the newscaster. "There's a name," he said.

"Wolf," Sandra repeated in a sinister voice. "Woooollf. Ahhooooooo." She bayed, or tried to, lifting her head. "Great name."

"I'm named for Pop," I told her. "Did you know that? Benjamin Joseph."

"Benjamin's a cool name," Sandra said. "But I like BJ okay."

"Do people call you Ben?" she asked Pop.

He nodded briefly, then looked at her with a sly grin. It was hard to believe that he was ninety-nine years old. He was cold all the time — I had to keep the heat turned up higher than was comfortable for me — and he slept a lot and used a cane. But his eyes were clear, his teeth mostly intact, and he still ate pizza.

"You ever know anybody named Toilet?" he asked her.

Sandra laughed. "Nope. I never even knew anyone named Wolf till tonight."

"Hot up my coffee, BJ," Pop said, gesturing toward the pot. I poured some more into the half-filled mug he'd been sipping.

"When I was a boy," Pop said, settling back in the chair, "right here on this farm, with a mess of brothers and sisters — none of them alive anymore; every one of them gone, but I could name them for you, in order — "

He paused and decided against it. "They sometimes would call me Ben Joe. For my name, see, for Benjamin Joseph."

Sandra nodded. "Ben Joe?" she mouthed at me, silently, with a look of amusement, and I had a feeling I had not heard the last of that name from her. But she continued listening politely to Pop.

"It's a southern-style thing, I think," he was saying. "Not usually New England. You know they got their Jim Bobs down south, along with their Bubbas?"

"Goodnight, Jim Bob," Sandra said, grinning at me.

"Goodnight, John-Boy," I replied.

Pop wasn't paying any attention. He had never watched *The Waltons*. He had lived like the Waltons, but he had never watched it on TV.

"But for some reason," he went on, ignoring us, "my sisters took it up for a while, when I was a kid. Ben Joe. I never liked it much, but they didn't mean no harm by it." He sipped his coffee again and rocked.

"And then, wouldn't you know, I was all grown up — married, had kids — and a nephew of mine came home after the war. That was WW Two. I didn't go off to it like some did. I was too young for the first war, too old for the second."

"I think my grandfather was in the Second World War," Sandra said. "He spent most of it on an island someplace. I'm pretty sure it was that war."

I leaned over and switched the television off since no one was listening. I glanced back at my French homework: uses of the subjunctive. Test on Friday. I'd heard the toilet story before.

"Who was that nephew, BJ? Do you remember his name? I think it must have been Clifford. My older sister's boy, Clifford. It was him." Pop nodded, getting his remembered facts together. "He came back here after the war to see his family and to get married. I don't know where he ended up after that. Think he went to Vermont or some darn place and made a mess of his life."

Actually, my Uncle Clifford had owned a motel in Vermont. His life hadn't been a mess, just a disappointment. He was retired now and divorced. One of his sons had run a motorcycle into a tree and was a paraplegic.

"But he'd been in Japan, see, after the war ended. He was in with the — what did they call it? — the Occupation forces. That's what Clifford did.

"And when he came back to the farm, he showed us all these here trinkets he'd brought back. He brought your father some, BJ. He was just a baby then.

"And he said to me that my name meant toilet in Japan. He had learned the language some, you see. And he said it was true: Ben Joe meant toilet. Not the same spelling, of course. They use that different style of writing in Japan, you know."

Sandra chuckled. "I wonder if my name means anything in Japanese," she said.

"Well, now, I couldn't say about that," Pop told her. "But I will tell you that no one ever called me Ben Joe after that."

"Of course they didn't," Sandra told him. She took his empty mug from him and carried it to the sink. "And Ben's a good name. I have to go, BJ. It's getting late. I'll see you tomorrow." She pulled her jacket on, gathered her books, and opened the kitchen door. "Yow, it's cold. Wind's starting up. I should have brought a hat."

It was November. No snow yet. I had just turned eighteen. The century would end in two months. Pop would have his one hundredth birthday in March. And in June 2000 I would graduate from high school.

I walked Sandra to her car, and when I went back to the kitchen I found Pop still talking.

"You'd think I'd never have a use for it," he told me in a loud voice.

"Use for what?" I added his mug to the dishwasher and reached under the sink for detergent.

"That name. Toilet!" He sputtered the word.

"Well, not unless you went to Japan. Then I guess you'd need to know what it meant. If you wanted a men's room, Pop, you'd be able to ask for it — "

He wasn't listening to me. He had become agitated, I could tell. He was plucking at the knees of his corduroy trousers, and one foot was tapping on the floor, his untied shoe moving up and down.

"Well, I did! I never told anybody this, BJ!" His foot tapped a quick, uneven beat on the pine boards.

"What, Pop?"

"That place. You know what I mean. That place there — " Angrily he gestured toward the doorway of the dark parlor, his hand waving. I did know what he meant.

"The prison."

"Those sons of bitches took my land!"

"They bought it, Pop. They paid you."

"Sons of bitches. They lied to me. They came here, knocked on my door. I let them in, thought they meant to be neighborly, thought we was going to talk about the — what was it, BJ, that they called it? The sanctuary, that's it. I was going to tell them about the place over by the creek where the fox had a den — "

He gestured, pointed, toward the place where once a

creek had run through the west pasture. "Jesus, BJ, I was going to tell them about the deer. Mornings, early — the moon would still be up, but the sky would lighten — and you could see a hundred deer grazing in that meadow. They'd move like dancers, in that silver light. I'd watch them from the window — "

I wondered on what day he had lowered the blinds and sealed forever the windows from which he had once watched deer.

"There was a pair of red-tailed hawks every spring. They'd nest high up. There was a clump of birches, oh, maybe thirty yards from the house. I could watch the hawks from the back porch. I used to sit there evenings, and they'd swoop out of that birch clump and soar up there against the sky, watching the fields for prey — "

I could hear the noise start. I glanced at my watch. It was almost ten. The noise always started about the same time. The banging. Someone was hitting metal on metal. I wondered, as I always did, what it was. A fork against a steel cell bar? A hundred forks?

"You said they came to the house, Pop."

He snorted. "I was prepared to advise them about the sanctuary. Was sitting here thinking about how I'd tell them the best ways to thin the deer herd. How to post the land against hunters. You know I hunted, BJ." He gestured toward the staircase, and I knew the gesture was reminding me of the gun cabinet, bolted to the wall in the upstairs hallway. "But never for sport. Only to thin the herd so there'd be no starvation. And sometimes I'd have to go after a predator.

"There was a fisher cat once. It was taking my chickens. I had to shoot the fisher — "

"Why did they come to the house, Pop?"

He shrugged, his skinny shoulders rising in the old plaid shirt: a gesture of defeat. "A courtesy, they told me. The courtesy of telling me they'd changed their minds, before I read it in the paper."

"They already owned the land? You'd sold it to them by then?"

He nodded. His eyes had a puzzled look. I calculated quickly in my mind. It had been almost twenty-five years before. Yet he was still puzzled: at what he had done, at what he had allowed them to do.

I loved him so much at that moment, when I saw his stricken, innocent eyes, when I saw his disbelief and that he did not understand betrayal, even in the midst of it.

The shouts started, now, on top of the banging. The howling and bellowing. Our windows were closed, but the noise came through the clear air and found ways inside the warm little room where my great-grandfather and I sat, so that his slow, puzzled speech was punctuated by the rage and obscenities of imprisoned men.

"They showed me the papers," he said. "They didn't need to. I remembered the papers I had signed at the lawyer's office. But they showed me my own signature. And that's when I told them about the name."

"The name?"

"I told them my name was Toilet," Pop said with a bitter, sardonic laugh.

They brought new prisoners in vans. They always had. Vans pulled through the gate, and you could, standing in the right spot in Pop's front yard, see through the fence to the place where they unloaded men chained at the feet so that their walk was a shuffle.

It had become startlingly frequent in recent months. Over the years I had seen the vans spit out the new prisoners occasionally; but in the past year it had become a steady, constant process. The local newspaper explained it: that the prison population had increased beyond any projections. They printed statistics: violent crime up, gun-related incidents up, rape at an all-time high, domestic murder at record proportions. It was like reading a weather report that told of hurricanes and blizzards beyond any known catastrophe of the past.

The overcrowded maximum-security prison in Collyerville, built in 1976 to hold four hundred, the newspaper said, now had a population of eight hundred and fifty men. The State Board of Corrections would be meeting to seek a solution.

I did not tell Pop.

Christmas slid by with its usual commercial celebration. My twelve-year-old sister showed off her new ice skates, and we ate turkey and cranberry sauce. I bundled Pop up and drove him to my house — though I hardly thought of it as mine, anymore — for the dinner Mom had cooked, and he fell asleep afterward in my father's old leather chair, wearing the new blue sweater from L. L. Bean that we had given him. We turned up the thermostat and arranged a blanket over him. Pop was always cold, now; and his feet, especially, were tinged with blue. The doctor said it was his poor circulation. Pop was ninety-nine years old.

Helping my mother with the dishes while Pop napped, I told her that I would postpone college in order to stay with him. She shook her head.

"You've got a life to start, BJ," she said. "We'll manage. I'll bring him here if he'll come. I'll hire someone to help out while I'm at work."

"I could sleep over with him next year," my sister said, looking up from where she was arranging her gifts — mittens, books, some jewelry — beside the boxed skates in a pile on the kitchen table.

"It probably won't be necessary," Mom said, glancing through the door at Pop's frail, cocooned shape in the big reclining chair. "We don't even need to think about it for a long time yet. It's only December."

"It's only 1999," my sister said. "Next week — whammo. Two thouuuusand. Two Oh Oh Oh."

"Oh Oh Oh," My mother and I replied, in unison. We startled ourselves.

*   *   *

Sandra came over on New Year's Eve. Practically everyone else in our little town was gathering, despite the bone-chilling cold, on the town green that night. My mother would be there, and my sister, bundled in down coats and fleece-lined boots like all of the townspeople, to watch the fireworks that would welcome the next century.

Pop was simply not up to such an excursion, and I didn't much care about it anyway. Sandra and I could watch the worldwide celebrations, surfing through everything from rock groups to solemn church services, on TV; and we would be able to see the town fireworks display from the porch.

We ate Kentucky Fried Chicken, turned on the news, and settled in. Heat steamed the windows of the house, but I could see that the thermometer attached to the pane over the kitchen sink was registering zero, its little red sliver of mercury contracted into a lump at the bottom of the tube.

Sandra and I rinsed out the little cardboard containers with their globs of coleslaw and cold potatoes, flattened them, and put them in the trash. We wrapped the uneaten chicken, stored it in the refrigerator — I knew I would eat it for breakfast — and I crumpled the greasy waxed paper from the cardboard bucket, along with our napkins. I loaded our plates and forks in the dishwasher, standing them next to the ones left from breakfast.

Pop dozed in his chair as he always did after supper. He

snored lightly. The newscaster, a woman, was interviewing a scholar about the meaning of the millennium. I reached over, clicked the channel changer, and the screen showed a church choir, mostly clear-skinned, rosy-cheeked little boys with neatly trimmed bangs; they were wearing white ruffles around their necks, like little girls playing dress up in their grandmothers' nightgowns. "*Sanctus*," they were singing in their high, perfect soprano voices. "*Sanctusssss.*" They drew the word out into a whisper and it trailed off, echoing in a cathedral somewhere. You could see people sitting motionless in the audience, holding their programs.

Holy. Holy. I recognized the Latin. So many words came from *sanctus*.

Sanctuary, I thought, and glanced over at Pop. He slept, still, his features calm.

"Should we put him to bed?" Sandra asked me.

But I shook my head. "He said he wanted to see it, wanted to see the century change. I'll just let him sleep, and then when the fireworks start, we can wake him up."

Sandra glanced at the frosted windows and shivered. "It's too cold out. We can't take him outside, not even to the porch, not even all bundled up."

"He can see from the windows," I told her.

And so we sat and waited, she and I. We sat on the couch near where Pop was slouched peacefully in his chair. Idly we clicked the cable channels to watch a comedian, a folksinger, a panel of scholars, all of them chortling, chanting, analyzing, all of them trying to figure out what it meant — or if it meant anything at all — to see the century slide into the past.

The noise began. The banging. It crossed my mind that even there, even in that crowded hell of a place, they might have planned some kind of celebration. I supposed that from their barred windows, even the caged men would see the fireworks. We turned the volume up, trying to drown the sounds from the prison without waking Pop. Aimlessly we watched reruns of old sitcoms from the fifties and sixties: Lucille Ball, Phil Silvers, Danny Thomas. All of that familiar, mindless humor and canned laughter.

Eventually Pop stirred. He yawned and asked for coffee. Then he sat silently, sipping at it. "What time is it?" he asked.

"Eleven," I told him. "The last hour of the century."

I changed the channel and found the familiar face of our local newscaster, anchorman from the capitol.

"On a more somber note," he was saying, "the State Board of Corrections has announced a bond issue to address the expansion of the penitentiary at Collyerville. In an ironic twist, it was announced today that the inmate population — now eight hundred and sixty-four — exceeds, for the first time, the population of that small, historic town in the northwest corner of the state."

I clicked MUTE. The three of us sat there in the silence, watching the anchorman's mouth move.

"I want to go upstairs," Pop said.

"It's only a little while to the fireworks, Pop. Don't you want to stay up for that?"

"Upstairs," he repeated. He was already rising slowly from his chair. I took his arm, supporting him from one side, and walked with him up to his room. I waited while he used the bathroom, then helped him with his clothes. He wore his long johns to bed. I put, clean, warm socks on his thin blue feet. I covered him with the thick quilt and kissed him on his veined forehead, smelling as I did the clean, musty aroma of his skin, thin as a moth's wing. It was the end of the century, but our small rituals were the same as any other night.

He said nothing. But he smiled at me.

Sandra had made us both a cup of fresh, steaming hot tea. When I came down, she handed me mine and told me it was almost time. So we layered ourselves with thick sweaters under our down jackets. We put on woolen hats and mittens and laced our boots over heavy socks. Even so, the air, when we opened the kitchen door to the porch, was a frigid blast that took our breath away for a moment.

The sky was awash with stars. Looking up, I had a sense of the world hurtling blindly, insignificantly, through the universe. We held hands and listened. The first thump of the explosions heralded the kaleidoscopic images above us; and then one after another, the dazzling eruptions appeared: ribbons of light bursting into monstrous blossoms that hung there and then wilted into fragments that fell, melting, to the horizon.

A peculiar phosphorescent light hung over the farmhouse and yard. Above us the sky continued to erupt in color, and the entire world continued to celebrate the end of something that none of us understood. We had left the television on, and through the kitchen door we could hear voices and cheers. We heard something else and didn't know what it was.

"Something's wrong," Sandra said suddenly to me.

I think that when my father was blinded by the sun and drove into the path of an oncoming train there must have been a moment of slow-motion awareness, a moment when he knew it was all too late to be changed, and he would have been filled not with fear but with surprise; and there would have, I think, been a moment, too, when a wild exhilaration overtook him and maybe he felt a great joy bursting forth because there was nothing, now, left for him to do but be taken; it was all out of his hands.

Running up the stairs, we found Pop's bed empty; and I was the one who noticed that the gun cabinet was open and empty, too.

I tried to raise the shade in his room: the shade that had been closed for twenty-four years. It resisted, and I tore it away from the window in shreds. From the window,

through that eerie phosphorescent light, I saw him standing there, almost a hundred years old, in his underwear,
green wool socks on his feet. I watch him raise the gun to
his frail, bony shoulder and shoot it again and again. I
watched him kill the Dobermans, his aim still as clear as it
had always been. Then I watched him shoot at the fences,
at the walls, at the watchtowers, at all the hated surfaces
that had blotched his beloved land for decades. I watched
the guards come, their guns drawn. He shot toward them,
and I saw them shoot, too, and some of their bullets hit
my Pop. But it didn't matter. By then his own rage and
passion had tunneled up through him and emerged, ex-
ploding in his heart like a peony coming into bright new
bloom.

Author's Note

Maybe it's because I'm getting older that I'm suddenly aware of how things are creeping up unan-
nounced. The ivy on my brick house seems to lie
dormant during the day, but somehow at night it
comes alive and I find it across the kitchen window in the morning, grabbing at the screen.

Armed with snippers, I can deal with the ivy.
But I feel other, more unmanageable things
creeping toward me as the century ends.

Here is what my local newspaper described
this morning: A woman kicked her baby daughter across the floor because she hadn't felt like
bending over to pick her up. A nursing aide was
charged with raping a comatose patient. An
anonymous bidder paid almost three million
dollars for a used baseball. Warplanes are going
at it over Iraq, and a buying frenzy is happening on Wall Street.

I feel violence and greed stalking me and shadowing my house.

I was feeling it when I sat down to write this story. So I dressed an old man in baggy underwear and sat him down in that shadow. We who write move the characters we create around on a stage built of our own experiences. Maybe in real life we, like the old man, pull down our shades and turn up the volume of the TV and drive in the other direction while we figure out how to deal with the stalkers. And maybe in real life we keep doing that forever. But on the story-stage, when the time comes, we go out in our baggy underwear and take action. We go out in the freezing cold against insurmountable opposition and we do what we have to do, even if it kills us.

I think this story is a statement about the strength, passion, and endurance of the human spirit. It is about fighting back against the threatening things that creep near.

THE LAST DOG

Katherine Paterson

Brock approached the customs gate. Although he did not reach for the scanner, a feeling it might have labeled "excitement" made him tremble. His fingers shook as he punched in his number on the inquiry board. "This is highly irregular, Brock 095670038," the disembodied voice said. "What is your reason for external travel?"

Brock took a deep breath. "Scientific research," he replied. He didn't need to be told that his behavior was "irregular." He'd never heard of anyone doing research outside the dome — actual rather than virtual research. "I — I've been cleared by my podmaster and the Research Team. . . . "

"Estimated time of return?" So, he wasn't to be questioned further.

"Uh, 1800 hours."

"Are you wearing the prescribed dry suit with helmet and gloves?"

"Affirmative."

"You should be equipped with seven hundred fifty milliliters of liquid and food tablets for one day travel."

"Affirmative." Brock patted the sides of the dry suit to be sure.

"Remember to drink sparingly. Water supply is limited." Brock nodded. He tried to lick his parched lips, but his whole mouth felt dry. "Is that understood?"

"Affirmative." Was he hoping customs would stop him? If he was, they didn't seem to be helping him. Well, this was what he wanted, wasn't it? To go outside the dome.

"Turn on the universal locator, Brock 095670038, and proceed to gate."

Why weren't they questioning him further? Were they eager for him to go? Ever since he'd said out loud in group speak that he wanted to go outside the dome, people had treated him strangely — that session with the podmaster and then the interview with the representative from Research. Did they think he was a deviant? Deviants sometimes disappeared. The word was passed around that they had "gone outside," but no one really knew. No deviant had ever returned.

The gate slid open. Before he was quite ready for it, Brock found himself outside the protection of the dome. He blinked. The sun — at least it was what was called "the sun" in virtual lessons — was too bright for his eyes even inside the tinted helmet. He took a deep breath, one last backward look at the dome, which, with the alien sun gleaming on it, was even harder to look at than the distant star, and started across an expanse of brown soil [was it?] to what he recognized from holograms as a line of purplish mountains in the distance.

It was, he pulled the scanner from his outside pouch and checked it, "hot." Oh, that was what he was feeling. Hot. He remembered "hot" from a virtual lesson he'd had once on deserts. He wanted to take off the dry suit, but he had been told since he could remember that naked skin would suffer irreparable burning outside the protection of the dome. He adjusted the control as he walked so that the unfamiliar perspiration would evaporate. He fumbled a bit before he found the temperature adjustment function. He put it on twenty degrees centigrade and immediately felt more comfortable. No one he really knew had ever left the dome, (stories of deviants exiting the dome being hard to verify), but there was all this equipment in case someone decided to venture out. He tried to ask the clerk who outfitted him, but the woman was evasive. The equipment was old, she said. People used to go out, but the outside environment was threatening, so hardly anyone (she looked at him carefully now), hardly anyone ever used it now.

Was Brock, then, the only normal person still curious about the outside? Or had all those who had dared to venture out perished, discouraging further forays? Perhaps he *was* a deviant for wanting to see the mountains for himself. When he'd mentioned it to others, they had laughed, but there was a hollow sound to the laughter.

If he never returned, he'd have no one to blame but himself. He knew that. While his podfellows played virtual games, he'd wandered into a subsection of the historical virtuals called "ancient fictions." Things happened in these fictions more — well, more densely than they did in the virtuals. The people he met there — it was hard to describe — but somehow they were more *actual* than dome dwellers. They had strange names like Huck Finn and M. C. Higgins the Great. They were even a little scary. It was their insides. Their insides were very loud. But even though the people in the ancient fictions frightened him a bit, he couldn't get enough of them. When no one was paying attention, he went back again and again to visit them. They had made him wonder about that other world — that world outside the dome.

Perhaps, once he had realized the danger the ancient fictions posed, he should have left them alone, but he couldn't help himself. They had made him feel hollow, hungry for something no food pellet or even virtual experience could satisfy. And now he was in that world they spoke of and the mountains of it were in plain view.

He headed for the purple curves. Within a short distance from the dome, the land was clear and barren, but after he had been walking for an hour or so he began to pass rusting hulks and occasional ruins of what might have been the dwellings of ancient peoples that no one in later years had cleared away for recycling or vaporization.

He checked the emotional scanner for an unfamiliar sensation. "Loneliness," it registered. He rather liked having names for these new sensations. It made him feel a bit "proud," was it? The scanner was rather interesting. He wondered when people had stopped using them. He hadn't known they existed until, in that pod meeting, he had voiced his desire to go outside.

The podmaster had looked at him with a raised eyebrow and a sniff. "Next thing you'll be asking for a scanner," he said.

"What's a scanner?" Brock asked.

The podmaster requisitioned one from storage, but at the same time, he must have alerted Research, because it was the representative from Research who had brought him the scanner and questioned him about his expressed desire for an Actual Adventure — a journey outside the dome.

"What has prompted this, uh — unusual ambition?"

the representative had asked, his eyes not on Brock but on the scanner in his hand. Brock had hesitated, distracted by the man's fidgeting with the strange instrument. "I — I'm interested in scientific research," Brock said at last.

So here he was out of the pod, alone for the first time in his life. Perhaps, though, he should have asked one of his podfellows to come along. Or even the pod robopet. But the other fellows all laughed when he spoke of going outside, their eyes darting back and forth. Nothing on the outside, they said, could equal the newest Virtual Adventure. He suddenly realized that ever since he started interfacing with the ancient fictions, his fellows had given him that look. They did think he was odd — not quite the same as a regular podfellow. Brock didn't really vibe with the pod robopet. It was one of the more modern ones, and when they'd programmed its artificial intelligence they'd somehow made it too smart. The robopet in the children's pod last year was older, stupider, and more "fun" to have around.

He'd badly underestimated the distance to the mountains. The time was well past noon, and he had at least three kilometers to go. Should he signal late return or turn about now? He didn't have much more than one day's scant supply of water and food tablets. But he was closer to the hills than to the dome. He felt a thrill ["excitement"] and pressed on.

There were actual trees growing on the first hill. Not the great giants of virtual history lessons, more scrubby and bent. But they were trees, he was sure of it. The podmaster had said that trees had been extinct for hundreds of years. Brock reached up and pulled off a leaf. It was green and had veins. In some ways it looked like his own hand. He put the leaf in his pack to study later. He didn't want anyone accusing him of losing his scientific objectivity. Only deviants did that. Farther up the hill he heard an unfamiliar burbling sound. No, he knew that sound. It was water running. He'd heard it once when the liquid dispenser had malfunctioned. There'd been a near panic in the dome over it. He checked the scanner. There was no caution signal, so he hurried toward the sound.

It was a — a "brook" — he was sure of it! Virtual lessons had taught that there were such things outside in the past but that they had long ago grown poisonous, then in the warming climate had dried up. But here was a running brook, not even a four-hour journey from his dome. His first impulse was to take off his protective glove and dip a finger in it, but he drew back. He had been well conditioned to avoid danger. He sat down clumsily on the bank. Yes, this must be grass. There were even some tiny flowers mixed in the grass. Would the atmosphere poison him if he unscrewed his helmet to take a sniff? He punched the scanner to read conditions, but the characters on the scanner panel danced about uncertainly until, at length, the disembodied voice said "conditions unreadable." He'd better not risk it.

He pushed the buttons now for liquid and pellets. A

tube appeared in his mouth. It dropped a pellet on his tongue. From the tube he sucked liquid enough to swallow his meal. What was it they called outside nourishment in the history virtuals? *Pecnec?* Something like that. He was having a *pecnec* in the *woods* by a *brook.* A hasty consulting of the scanner revealed that what he was feeling was "pleasure." He was very glad he hadn't come with an anxious podfellow or, worse, an advanced robopet that would, no doubt, be yanking at his suit already, urging him back toward the dome.

It was then, in the middle of post-*pecnec* satisfaction, that he heard the new sound. Like that programmed into a robopet, yet different. He struggled to his feet. The dry suit from storage was certainly awkward when you wanted to stand up or sit down. Nothing on the scanner indicated danger, so he went into the scrubby woods toward the sound. And stopped abruptly.

Something was lying under the shadow of a tree. Something about a meter long. It was furred and quite still. The sound was not coming from it. And then he saw the small dog — the puppy. He was sure it was a puppy, nosing the stiff body of what must once have been its mother, making the little crying sounds that he'd heard from the brook. Later, much later, he realized that he should have been wary. If the older dog had died of some extradomal disease, the puppy might have been a carrier. But at the time, all he could think of was the puppy, a small creature who had lost its mother.

He'd found out about mothers from the Virtuals. Mothers were extinct in the dome. Children were conceived and born in the lab and raised in units of twelve in the pods, presided over by a bank of computers and the podmaster. Nuclear families, as everyone knew, had been wasteful of time, energy, and space. There was an old proverb: The key to survival is efficiency. So though Brock could guess the puppy was "sad" (like that fictions person, Jo, whose podmate expired), he didn't know what missing a mother would feel like. And who would whimper for a test tube?

Brock had never seen a dog, of course, but he'd had seen plenty of dog breed descriptions on the science/history virtuals. Dogs had been abundant once. They filled the ancient fictions. They even had names there — Lassie, Toto, Sounder. But now dogs were extinct, gone during the dark ages when the atmosphere had become warm and poisonous. The savages who had not had the intelligence or wealth to join the foresighted dome crafters had killed all animals wild or domesticated for food before they had eventually died out themselves. It was all in one of the very first virtual lessons. He had seen that one many times. He never confessed to anyone how, well, sad it made him feel.

But obviously, dogs were not quite extinct. Cautiously, he moved toward the small one.

"Alert. Alert. Scanning unknown object."

Brock pushed the off button. "Are you sure you want to turn off scanner?"

"Affirmative." He stuck the scanner into his pouch.

The puppy had lifted its head at the sound of his voice. It looked at him, head cocked, as though deciding whether to run or stay.

"It's all right, dog," Brock said soothingly. "I won't hurt you." He stayed still. He didn't want to frighten the little beast. If it ran, he wasn't sure he'd be able to catch it in his clumsy dry suit.

Slowly he extended his gloved hand. The dog backed away anxiously, but when Brock kept the hand extended, the puppy slowly crept toward him and sniffed, making whimpering sounds. It wasn't old enough to be truly afraid, it seemed. The pup licked his glove tentatively, then backed away again. It was looking for food, and plasticine gloves weren't going to satisfy.

Brock looked first at the dead mother whose source of nourishment must have long dried up, then around the landscape. What would a dog eat? A puppy on its own? He took off his glove and reached through his pouch into the inside pocket that held his pellet supply. Making every move slow and deliberate so as not to startle the dog, he held out a pellet. The dog came to his hand, licked it, then the pellet. It wrinkled its nose. Brock laughed. He didn't need the scanner now to tell him that what he felt was "pleasure." He loved the feel of the rough tongue on his palm and the little furred face, questioning him.

"It's all right, fellow. You can eat it."

As though understanding, the pup gulped down the pellet. Then looked around for more, not realizing that it had just bolted down a whole meal. When the dog saw there was no more coming, it ran over to the brook. Brock watched in horror as it put its head right down into the poisonous stream and lapped noisily.

"Don't!" Brock cried.

The puppy turned momentarily at the sound, then went back to drinking, as though it was the most normal thing in the world. Well, it was, for the dog. Where else would a creature in the wild get liquid? If the streams were not all dried up, they must have learned to tolerate the water. But then, it was breathing the poisoned atmosphere, wasn't it? Why hadn't it hit Brock before? This was a fully organic creature on the outside *without any life support system*. What could that mean? Some amazing mutation must have occurred, making it possible for at least some creatures to breath the outside atmosphere and drink its poisoned water. Those who couldn't died, those who could survived and got stronger. Even the ancient scientist Darwin knew that. And Brock had come upon one of these magnificent mutants!

The puppy whimpered and looked up at Brock with large, trusting eyes. How could he think of it as a mutant specimen? It was a puppy. One who had lost its mother. What would it eat? There was no sign of food for a carnivore. Perhaps way back in the mountains some small mammals had also survived, keeping the food chain going, but the puppy would not live long enough to find its way there, much less know how to hunt with its mother gone. For the first time in his life something deep inside Brock reached out toward another creature. The thought of the puppy languishing here by the side of its dead parent until it, too . . .

"Your name is Brog, all right?" The ancient astronomers had named stars after themselves. He had discovered something just as wonderful. Didn't he have the right to name it sort of after himself while preserving the puppy's uniqueness? "Don't worry, Brog. I won't let you starve."

Which is why Brock appeared at the customs portal after dark, the front of his dry suit stained, carrying a wriggling *Canis familiaris* of uncertain breed.

If there had been any way to smuggle the dog in, Brock would have. But he couldn't for the life of him figure out how. As it was, every alarm in the area went off when he stepped into the transitional cubicle. The disembodied voice of the monitor queried him:

"Welcome back, Brock 095670038. You're late."

"Affirmative."

"And you are carrying contraband."

"I pulled a leaf."

"Deposit same in quarantine bins."

"Affirmative."

"Sensors denote warm-blooded presence not on official roster."

"I found a dog," Brock mumbled.

"Repeat."

"A dog."

"*Canus familiaris* is extinct."

"Well, maybe it's just a robopet that got out somehow."

"Correction. Robopets are bloodless. Leave dry suit for sterilization and proceed to quarantine inspection."

The officials in quarantine inspection, who rarely had anything to inspect, were at first nervous and then, as they watched the puppy happily licking Brock's face, interested despite themselves. An actual dog! None of them had ever seen one, of course, and Brock's dog was so much, well, more vital than a robopet. And although, on later reflection, they knew they should have terminated or expelled it, they couldn't quite bring themselves to do so that night.

"It will have to go to Research," the chief inspector finally declared.

"Permission requested to hand carry the dog known as Brog to Research," Brock said. There was a bit of an argument about that. Several inspectors sought the honor, but the chief declared that Brock, having shed his dry suit and being already contaminated, should be placed with the dog in a hermetically sealed air car and transported to Research.

The scientists in Research were predictably amazed to see a live *Canis familiaris*. But being scientists and more objective than the lower-grade quarantine inspectors, they kept a safe distance both physically and psychically from the creature. Only the oldest scientist, dressed in proper protective clothing, came into the laboratory with Brock and the dog. He scanned and poked and prodded the poor little fellow until it began to whimper in protest.

"Brog needs to rest," said Brock, interrupting the scientist in the midst of his inspection. "She's (for by this time gender had been indisputably established) had a hard day. And if there's some actual food available — she's not used to pellets."

"Of course, of course," said one of the researchers through the speaker in the observation booth. "How thoughtless. Send someone out for a McLike burger without sauce. She may regard it as meat. Anyhow, it will seem more like food to her than a pellet, affirmative, Brock?"

The scientists, Brock soon realized, were looking to him for advice. He was, after all, the discoverer of the last dog. It gave him sudden scientific status. Brock had sense enough to take advantage of this. After Brog had swallowed the McLike burger in three quick gulps, Brock insisted that he be allowed to stay with Brog, so that he might interact and sleep with her. "She's not like us," he explained. "She's used to tumbling about and curling up with other warm bodies. In the old myths," he added, "puppies separated from their litters cried all night long. She will need constant interaction with another warm-blooded creature or she might well die of," he loved using his new vocabulary, "'loneliness.'"

The scientists agreed. After all, research was rather like quarantine, and since Brock had touched the dog ungloved and unprotected, he might well have picked up some germ from her. It was better to keep them both isolated in the research lab where proper precautions would be taken.

For nearly a week, Brock lived with Brog in the research center, eating McLike burgers, playing "fetch," teaching Brog to "sit," "heel," "come" — all the commands he could cull from the ancient texts. The dog quickly learned to obey Brock's commands, but it wasn't the automatic response of a robopet. Brog delighted in obedience. She wanted to please Brock, and those few times when she was too busy nosing about the lab and failed to obey instantly, those times when Brock's voice took on a sharp tone of reproof, the poor little thing put her tail between her legs, looked up at him with sorrowful eyes, begging to be forgiven. Brock was tempted to speak sharply to her even when there was no need, for the sight of her drooping ears and tail, her mournful eyes was so dear to him that he did what Travis Coates had done to Old Yeller. He hugged her. There was no other way to explain it. He simply put his arms around her and held her to his chest while she beat at him with her tail and licked his face raw. Out of the corner of his eye he was aware that one of the scientists was watching. Well, let him watch. Nothing was as wonderful as feeling this warmth toward another creature.

For the first week, the researchers seemed quite content to observe dog and boy from their glass-paneled observation booth and speak copious notes into their computers. Only the oldest of them would come into the lab and actually touch the alien creature, and he always wore a sterile protective suit with gloves. The others claimed it would interfere with objectivity if they got close to the dog, but they all seemed to behave positively toward Brog. No mention was made to Brock of his own less than objective behavior. So Brock was astounded to awake in the middle of the night to the sounds of an argument. Someone had forgotten to turn off the communication system.

"Cloning — it's the only thing to do. If she's the last, we owe it to posterity to keep the line going."

"And how are we going to raise a pack of dogs in a dome? One is nearly eating and drinking us out of test tube and petri dish. We can't go on this way. As drastic as it may seem, we have to be realistic. Besides, no one has had the chance to do actual experiments since the dark ages. Haven't you ever, just once, yearned to compare virtual research with actual?"

"What about the boy? He won't agree. Interfacing daily with the dog, he's become crippled by primal urges."

"Can you think what chaos might ensue if a flood of primordial emotions were to surface in a controlled environment such as ours?" another asked. "Apparently, emotions are easily triggered by interactions with primitive beasts, like dogs."

"Shh. Not now. The speaker is — " The system clicked off.

But Brock had already heard. He knew he had lost anything resembling scientific objectivity. He was no longer sure objectivity was a desirable trait. He rather enjoyed being flooded by "primordial emotions." But he was more worried for Brog than for himself. It wasn't hard to figure out what the scientists meant by "actual experiments." Cloning would be bad enough. Ten dogs who looked just like Brog so no one would know how special, how truly unique Brog was. But experiments! They'd cut her open and examine her internal organs, the way scientists had in the dark ages. They'd prod her with electric impulses and put chips in her brain. They'd try to change her personality or modify her behavior. They'd certainly try to make her eat and drink less!

In the dark, he put his arm around Brog and drew her close. He loved the terrible smell of her breath and the way she snored when she slept. They'd probably fix that, too.

The next day he played sick. Brog, faithful dog that she was, hung around him whimpering, licking his face. The scientists showed no particular concern. They were too busy plotting what they might do with Brog.

Brock crept to the nearest terminal in the lab. It was already logged in. The scientists had been doing nothing but research on *Canis familiaris*. COMMON CANINE DISEASES. Brock scrolled down the list with descriptions. No, *distemper* wouldn't do. The first symptom was loss of appetite. He couldn't make Brog fake that. On and on it went — no, *heartworms* wouldn't do. What he needed was a disease that might affect *Homo sapiens* as well as *Canis familiaris*. Here it was! "Rabies: A viral disease occurring in animals and humans, esp. in dogs and wolves. Transmitted by bite or scratch. The early stages of the disease are most dangerous, for an otherwise healthy and friendly appearing animal will suddenly bite without provocation."

Rabies was it! Somehow he would have to make Brog bite him. There was no antirabies serum in the dome, he felt sure. There were no animals in the dome. Why would they use precious space to store an unneeded medication? So they'd have to expel him as well as Brog for fear of spreading the disease. He shivered, then shook himself. No matter what lay on the outside, he could not stand to go back to the life he had lived in the dome before he met Brog.

He crept back to bed, pulling the covers over Brog. When one of the scientists came into the observation booth, Brock pinched Brog's neck as hard as he could. Nothing. He pinched again, harder. Brog just snuggled closer, slobbering on his arm.

Disgusted, Brock got out of bed. Brog hopped down as well, rubbing against his leg. Pinching obviously was not going to do it. While the scientist on duty in the booth was bending over a computer terminal, Brock brought his foot down on Brog's paw. A tiny *yip* was all he got from that cruel effort — not enough sound even to make the man look up.

"Feeling better, Brock 095670038?" The oldest researcher had come into the lab.

"Affirmative," Brock answered.

"And how are you, puppy-wuppy?" The old man tickled Brog under her chin with his gloved hand. *If I were a dog, I'd bite someone like that,* thought Brock, but Brog, of course, simply licked the researcher's glove and wagged her tail.

That was when he got his great idea. He waited to execute it until the proper moment. For the first time, all the scientists had gathered in the lab, all of them in protective garb, some of them twitching nervously in their chairs. They were sitting in a circle around Brock and Brog, explaining what must be done.

"It has to be done for the sake of science," they began. Then they went on to, "For the sake of the dome community, which is always, as you well know, short on food, and particularly short on water." Brock listened to their arguments, nodding solemnly, pretending to agree. "It won't be as if she'll really be gone, you know. We've made virtuals of her — a special series just for you to keep. You can virtually play with her whenever you like."

That was the cue. Brock turned and bit Brog on the tail so hard that the blood started. Brog, surprised and enraged, spun around and bit Brock on the nose.

There was a shocked silence. Every scientist leaned

backward, body pressed hard against his or her chair back. Every eye was on the two of them.

"I — I don't know what got into me," Brock said. "I've been feeling very weird." The scientists continued to stare. "I was checking the historical records. . . . "

All of the scientists fled the room. Someone ran to a computer terminal. When Brock offered to take Brog out of the dome and let her loose in the mountains, no one argued. Neither did they say, "Hurry back," or even, "Take care." No one came close as he loaded his pouch with water and food pellets. The customs gate monitor asked no questions.

Out of sight of the dome, Brog was delirious with joy, jumping and running about in circles around Brock's boots. Why wasn't the atmosphere choking Brog if it was as poisonous as the dome dwellers claimed? His heart beating rapidly, Brock unscrewed his helmet just enough to let in a little of the outside atmosphere. Nothing happened. In fact, he seemed to be breathing perfectly normally. He took off the helmet entirely. He was still breathing freely. But his heart was beating so hard, he couldn't be sure. He waited for the choking sensation he had been warned of. It didn't occur. Could they be wrong? Could the outside world have healed itself? Perhaps — perhaps the reason the scanner had so much trouble reading the outside atmosphere was because it wasn't within the range of computerized expectations.

Could it be? Could it be that fear had kept the dome dwellers prisoner many years longer than a poisoned environment would have?

He unfastened the dry suit and slowly stepped out of it into the sunlight.

It was wonderful how much faster he could walk without the clumsy suit. "Who knows?" Brock said to a frisking Brog. "Who knows, maybe out here you aren't the last dog. Your mother had to come from somewhere."

Brog barked happily in reply.

"And maybe, just maybe, where there are dogs, there are humans as well."

They stopped at the brook where they'd met, and both of them had a long drink. Brock no longer carried a scanner, but he knew what he felt was excitement. The water was delicious.

Author's Note

When Michael Cart asked me to write a story for this collection, I replied, "But, Michael, I write historical fiction. I haven't caught up with the twentieth century yet." He asked me to try, so I did, but it seemed hopeless. Besides, I was going to Australia, and I just didn't have time to worry about a story set in the unknown future.

I was speaking in a school in Melbourne when I got the inevitable question: Where do you get your ideas? "Wherever I can find them," I said. "Take this morning, for example. I was looking out the hotel window at an expanse of green, which I thought must be a cricket field. A man was mowing the grass on a rider mower, and trotting right behind him right in the track of the back right wheel was a mongrel dog.

"The way the dog was following so faithfully

behind the mower made me think that the groundskeeper was the dog's master. Finally, the mower got to the end of the field and turned to go back. The dog stopped at the end of his little track. He seemed quite confused. His track had disappeared. He looked around for a minute, then trotted over to a bush and lifted his leg. His business taken care of, he slid under the fence, out of the park, and disappeared up the sidewalk, headed for his next adventure of the day.

"Now, someone," I said, "could make a story of that dog. Even from the distance of a hotel window, I could tell he was quite a wonderful creature."

I went back to the hotel and thought about my dog of the morning, which led to thinking of all the dogs of my life and how I missed having a dog and, well, suppose in a polluted, damaged world there were no dogs. That was too sad to think about for long, so I began to imagine a boy who came upon what seemed to be the very last dog on earth.

THE OTHER HALF OF ME

Jacqueline Woodson

And it has always begun in the middle — me coming fast in the middle of the night and even before that — the first morning my mother sat down to figure out how to make the dream of me come true. The middle of her life, she says. A point where she could have gone either way, and everyone thinking she was too old to have me, too old to start making plans. And alone.

There had been men who had loved her and men she had loved. I imagine her sitting down in a café remembering the ones who had moved their hands through her hair and stared into her eyes. The men who had come into her life for weeks and months and years at a time. But they were behind her now.

As she sat sipping her coffee and going through pages and pages of donor information, she remembered the ones she had approached. Maybe she'd said, "I want to have a baby," and the men had stared back, wide-eyed, stammering about how they weren't ready to be fathers, how the decision was more than they could — "No," my mother must have said. "I don't want you to be the father." And the stammering men, one by one, apologized, gave weak reasons about ideas of true love, whole families, and the influence of male role models. Even the grown sons of single mothers forgot, in the moment of my mother's asking, how they themselves had come into the world. "But there are male role models everywhere," my mother had said. "In my life and in the world." But the men shook their heads, said they weren't ready to be fathers. And my mother shook her own head, saying again, "I'm not asking you to be." One by one until there was no ex-boyfriend or friend left to ask.

They didn't understand, she would tell me years later, that there were other ways of being, of being a family, of being whole. They couldn't wrap their minds around the idea of my dream of you, of something different, another way.

But there *were* other ways.

As my mother sat dreaming of me, she read the statements of donors, looked closely at their physical descriptions, discarding men because of the straightness of their hair, the curve of their nose, their ideas about family. Yes, I was my mother's dream, her "one day" — existing in a future she could *just* imagine: Me in her arms. Me across her shoulder, my head nestled into her neck. Me asleep beside her, my baby breath warm and sweet. And later, as she called friends who knew friends who had come by their children the way my mother was planning to come by me, the visions and dreams of me became more real, more clear. Some mornings, she'd lie with her eyes closed and the wind blowing just so across the back of her neck. And there I was, behind her lids, a tiny boy with a head of wet black hair and hands curling into fists, my mouth open in a yawn.

But I was not a boy, I remind her. *And my eyes. What color were they?*

She frowns and tells me that at first they were blue-gray, then brown as tea. That when they began to darken, it was clear I was her child. Then I was no longer some faraway dream. I was me.

But my eyes aren't brown, I say. *You were still dreaming.*

And she smiles and says, *But you were closer.*

The years passed and the stories changed. Or maybe my mother changed. *You were born with your eyes open. No, maybe they were closed. Your grandfather was afraid to hold you at first. It was your grandfather who was the first after me to hold you.*

We moved. And then we moved again. *I don't feel settled here*, my mother would say, resting her hand on her belly. *This place isn't calling my name.*

In Canada, a stranger touched my mother's belly, then examined both of my mother's hands. "But you're not married," the stranger said.

Canada, my mother says, wasn't calling her name.

And years later, in Colorado, a man eyed my mother and me as we walked side by side along a street I no longer remember. That night, that same man showed up at our door. "It's just the two of you, isn't it?" he asked.

And so we moved again. As the world got closer to us, we packed what little we owned and left it behind.

"We'll find a place one day," my mother promised when I was nine. "Someplace that feels as though it's wrapping us in its arms. . . ."

"And calling our names," I said.

"Calling our names," my mother echoed, pulling me closer to her.

We were not running away, we were walking home. It was a long walk, one that would take years. But we'd get there. We knew we would.

But for a long time there was no real world, just blurs and blurs of towns and people: A tiny red-doored store with an old-fashioned Pepsi sign nailed above its window. A tulip-filled town called Tiptoe. A pretty girl in Oregon who sat with her hands folded at recess. A boy with a bump where a sixth finger used to be in Cape May. A small black dog in Orleans, Massachusetts, that came to us one winter evening in the rain and left the following spring.

Or maybe we left.

There were my mother's parents in New Hope, Pennsylvania, and second grade in a tiny brown schoolhouse that was founded by Quakers. There was my grandfather with me on his lap listening as he read *Goodnight Moon* over and over until I was asleep. *Goodnight Moon* — too young for me but familiar as my grandfather's warm, brown hands, the words coming from his mouth, lulling as a song.

" — And Todd," I say when my mother and I are sitting at the table, drinking homemade milk shakes and remembering. "Your once boyfriend named Todd."

"Once," my mother says. "A long time ago."

"But it wasn't him."

My mother looks at me and shakes her head. "You know it wasn't Todd."

"But it could have been."

"Yes," my mother says. "It could have been. But it wasn't."

"Because Todd said no," I say.

"Because Todd said no."

"And the others said no, too."

My mother looks at me and smiles. "And I'm glad they did. Because then you wouldn't be you, would you?"

I shake my head. "Then who?"

"You know who, Reverie. You know as much as I know."

I know I was born on an island off the coast of Maine. Swan's Island. The house I was born in had been built at the turn of the century. The woman who delivered me had brown hands — strong and able, my mother said, and that's why she wasn't afraid. Because the only brown things on Swan's Island were Mama and that woman's hands. And when I ask about the rest of the woman, my mother doesn't remember. She says she sees even now only a white woman with brown hands. And maybe there are reasons, she says. Maybe the woman had spent her life dying the wool of the sheep her husband raised. Wool that was sheared and cleaned and woven and shipped to Vermont and Massachusetts and New York where it was knitted and purled and crocheted into beautiful sweaters grandmothers made for their not yet born grandchildren. Or maybe the woman worked the land so hard and long that her hands sipped up the color of the earth as easily as milk moved through paper straws. *I don't know*, my mother says. *But that night there was only me and that woman's hands. The only brown on the whole island. And then you. Pale and fussy at first, but eventually you, too, were brown. And we stayed there a while.*

I was born without a father. I am what people call an outside girl. A donor baby. My mother's one-woman show. My father is a file locked inside my mother's safety deposit box. Donor number 5364, the file says. African American. 6′2″. 180 lbs. Age 25. Student. Medicine. Piano and flute player. Can the child contact you at 18?

— No.

What message would you give to the child?

— Let the world know where you stand. Don't ever be a coward.

Why have you chosen not to be identified?

[The donor has intentionally left this section blank.]

The donor was interviewed at 12:30 P.M. on Monday, November 17, 19__. He is warm, has an easy smile. . . .

Even then I began in the middle — a man walking into a sperm bank in California, mid-twenties, broke. Midday.

Maybe he held his hat in his hands. Asking questions. Being asked questions. Whispering the answers that were too embarrassing to say out loud. *Why are you donating?* A nurse may have asked him. And in the file, this question is left blank — which means it was for the money, my mother says.

"Why would you pick someone who only did it for the money?" But what I really want to know is what makes my father smile easily. What makes him laugh and cry. And as I dip my head toward my mother waiting for an answer, is he somewhere in the world dipping his head the same way? "Why?" I ask again.

And my mother looks down at her hands and says, "Because he said to let the world know where you stand."

"But he was too afraid to even know me? He didn't want to *know* me."

I am a girl, Daddy. I am Reverie. I have your eyes.

And my mother keeps staring at her hands. "You were a long time coming, Reverie. Sometimes the wanting outweighs the thinking. What mattered then was that there was someone else out there who thought that we should be true to ourselves — and to the world. And that you were closer to being here."

I began as my mother's dream of me. In the middle of her thinking.

There is a file in my mother's safety deposit box that is rubbed raw and smeared and very much handled. It is my father — in black and white and now yellowing around the edges. My father — a sheaf of papers in a manila folder. My father — he has never been hospitalized, the file says. He has a brother and two sisters. He eats at least two servings of fruit each day, takes vitamins, exercises. He likes soccer, taking apart cars and putting them together again. He was born into Christianity. His hair is curly and his skin is dark. His eyes are green. No family history of sickle cell. And the year I was born he was in medical school.

I don't know where he was born. I know the sperm that would become me was shipped from California to Boston where my mother was living at the time. I know it was kept cold with dry ice. I know my mother wanted a girl even though she dreamed the baby would be a boy. I know my mother wanted me. Her daughter. Her Reverie.

And I know I've always been searching, from the first moment I looked into my mother's eyes. Even though I didn't know it, couldn't speak or reach out and call his name. I know I've always been turning corners and looking over my shoulders and staring men down. Looking for my father. Looking for the other half of me.

And I have found me everywhere: green-eyed men driving trucks that passed us on the highway, dark-skinned men with my own curling hair, pale men with sharp noses and high cheekbones.

In a small town, just outside of Albany, there was a man on a bus. A dark, curly-haired man with my eyes and mouth. A man who turned and saw me and smiled. And I stood there, my hair blowing into my face, my hands deep in the pockets of my jeans. Until the bus pulled away. Until the dust of his smile was all that remained.

It is summer now and soon I'll be fifteen. Outside, the sun settles down bright red and gold. There is no wind but the sound of crickets chirping carries over to us. A frog groans somewhere. A bird. Under the porch there are five black-and-gray kittens, the mother gone. What I want this evening is to hear the tale again, how I came into the world almost completely true to her dream but a girl — a bald girl whose hands were wide open and palm-side up as though I was reaching for life, grabbing it, she said. And holding on. What I want is the man from Albany sitting at this table with us, telling me about his life, my life. His family, my family.

We have been here a long time. Our house is near a lake and far away from other houses. The world leaves us alone. Now, my mother looks out the window and smiles. She says she thinks this is a place she'd like to stay for a while. There is a school here, she says. And work in the town.

Some evenings my mother and I are complete as bookends. Whole. Complementing.

Tonight, as my mother speaks softly about staying here a while, I let myself fall into the rhythm of her voice, the tomorrow she promises me. The man in Albany's smile lifts up from the dust and swirls slowly around me. Maybe this will be the place he will come to find me.

"Yes," I say to mother. "Yes, let's stay here a while."

Author's Note

Growing up in a single-mom household, I was intrigued as a child by the idea of "father." I didn't actually meet my biological dad until I was fifteen, at which point he and my mom decided they wanted to be a couple again. Up until I met him, I had fantasies about who he was, and like Reverie, I, too, believed I caught glimpses of him everywhere.

It wasn't until years later that I realized my mom had been both mother and father to me and that I had gotten all the tools I needed to be whole in the world from her and from the many other strong people surrounding me. Reverie is a bit of who I was before I realized this.

Recently I read that in the year 2000, the first children of known donors (donors who have said okay to being identified) will turn eighteen and have a chance to meet the donor. (I use the word "donor" here rather than "father" because I think these words imply different things.) This story was also inspired by that piece of information and by the fact that I am in touch with so many different kinds of families, including children of single mothers, children with two mothers and/or two fathers, children whose parents are divorced, and children whose parents are together. I have learned in my time on this earth that there are so many ways to be a family. As I write, until I write the last line, I don't know where my characters will end up or who they'll be when they get there. But some part of me knows that, in the end, Reverie will be all right.

NIGHT OF THE PLAGUE

James Cross Giblin

Water! Please! Water!" The child's voice came from the cot at the end of the room. It was so weak, so thin, that Anthony almost didn't hear it.

Before the young monk could comply with the child's request, a bony hand reached out from another cot and clutched his robe. Startled, Anthony swung around. He thought he had seen all there was to see of human suffering, but the old woman's face still made him gasp. It was covered with large, purplish spots that had not been there the hour before, and the woman's eyes oozed a yellowish fluid.

"Help me, Brother," she whispered. "My face is on fire. I can't see. I can't breathe!"

"Water!" the child called again, but Anthony ignored his plea for the moment. He couldn't help two people at once. The young monk went to a small table between the woman's cot and the next one and dipped a cloth in a bowl of water.

"The cloth is hot," the woman complained when Anthony gently bathed her face with it.

"No," he said reassuringly. "It's your face that's hot — the cloth is cool. Be patient. Soon you will feel its coolness — "

Anthony stopped speaking when the woman's eyes suddenly opened wide with a look of pure fear. The purple blotches on her face seemed to darken as she raised her head jerkily. "Ah-h-h-h-h-h-h!" she shrieked in a voice so loud that it woke all the sleepers in the room. Then, as Anthony watched helplessly, the woman's head fell back, the color faded from her face, and she lay motionless on the narrow cot.

Without examining her, Anthony knew that she was dead. He had seen too many people die in the last month not to recognize the signs. His heart ached with grief at yet another death, but he kept his emotions to himself. What good would more sobs do? He had sobbed so much already.

A hushed silence filled the room as Anthony pulled the woman's thin blanket up over her body. None of the other patients asked what had happened; like Anthony, they all knew. The stronger ones rose up on their elbows and watched the monk close the woman's eyelids and bow his head in prayer. The weaker ones could do no more than lie back and wonder when their hour would come. Only the child, far off in the corner, raised his voice. "Water!" he cried again.

Anthony nodded to another monk, Brother Paul, who was sitting on guard by the doorway. Then Anthony rose wearily and headed in the child's direction. Meanwhile, Brother Paul walked over to the old woman's cot and lifted her body into his arms. He would take away the body and bury it in the monastery graveyard with all the other victims of the plague.

The child in the corner was a new patient. Someone else — a gnarled old man — had lain in his cot when Anthony had made his rounds earlier that evening. The man must have died while Anthony was eating supper. As the young monk drew near, he realized with a start that the child wasn't much younger than he. Anthony had turned sixteen on his last birthday, and this boy looked to be thirteen, maybe even fourteen.

Anthony poured water into a mug from a clay pitcher and approached the boy slowly. The fact that they were almost the same age made it harder somehow for Anthony to care for him. It was too easy to imagine himself lying there, so thin and pale. So close to death. The boy lifted himself painfully to take a sip of the water. But he began to choke when he tried to swallow it. Anthony reached out to support him and felt his shoulder bone beneath the skin; there was almost no flesh left on his body.

The boy fixed his brown eyes on Anthony and asked the question the young monk had been asking himself ever since the plague had struck. "Is this the end of the world?"

If Anthony hadn't been so tired, he might have been able to answer the boy with soothing words. But he'd been working day and night for weeks now, helping to feed, wash, and nurse the hundreds of sick people who had fled to the monastery. They'd hoped to escape the plague that was ravaging the city in the valley; instead, they'd brought the dread disease with them.

"Is it?" the boy asked again. He was longing for reassurance, for a reason to hope. But what hope could Anthony offer him? The young monk was filled with doubt himself. "I don't know," he mumbled at last. "I don't know."

The boy shuddered and fell back on the cot. Not looking at Anthony, he said simply, "I'm so afraid."

Anthony longed to kneel beside the boy, take his hand, and say, "Do not fear, my son. God is looking after you. Whatever happens on this earth, He will lead you into a better life in Heaven." That's what the older monks would have said. That's what they had said to Anthony when he had expressed his own doubts and fears to them.

But Anthony wasn't sure enough of his beliefs to repeat

their words to this boy. Maybe he was too young, maybe he simply hadn't lived long enough. Or maybe — and this was the most frightening thought of all — he was a bad person who would never know the blessing of God's love.

While these thoughts tumbled through Anthony's mind, the boy heaved a huge sigh and then lay still. Had he, too, died? Anthony did not want to find out. It was cowardly of him, he knew, but he had seen too much of suffering and death in these past weeks. All he wanted — all he could think of — was to get away from it. To flee the cries and pleas and dying gasps of the plague victims.

He looked around the infirmary. Brother Paul had not returned from the graveyard, and no other monks were in the dimly lit room. For once, all the patients were quiet, either asleep or too weak to make a sound. With no one clamoring for his attention and no other monks to see what he did, it would be a perfect time for Anthony to slip away.

He had no idea where he was going as he left the infirmary. But wherever he went he would need his woolen cloak to fend off the strong winter winds. After glancing up and down the narrow, stone-floored hall, he hurried up a flight of stairs to his small cell on the floor above. He grabbed his cloak from the peg where it hung, then paused for a moment to look at the wooden cross on the wall next to his bed. If only his beliefs were as strong as those of Brother Paul and the other monks. . . .

Downstairs again, he surveyed the hall once more before darting out through the door at the far end. The wind hit him full in the face as he struggled along the path that led away from the monastery. Clutching his cloak more tightly about him, he headed toward the monastery's pond. It lay at the foot of a hill, and there was a rough wooden shelter beside it where he could rest out of the wind while he decided what to do next.

He sank onto the bench inside the shelter and stared at the pond. Tonight, under a full moon, its usually placid surface was whipped into waves by the wind. How different it had looked last summer when Brother Paul had first led Anthony to it. Then, dragonflies flitted through the air, and a bright afternoon sun carpeted the surface of the water with a thousand sparkling jewels.

Anthony, newly arrived from the city, had smiled delightedly as he surveyed the scene. He and Brother Paul had laughed when two male geese got into a squabble, honking loudly at each other, flapping their wings, and spraying water everywhere. Who could have imagined on that carefree afternoon that within a few short months a terrible plague would sweep across the country, enveloping the city and spreading to the monastery?

Anthony could not go back to the city, even if he had wanted to. He had no family there — his parents had died in a flood more than five years ago, and the grandmother with whom he had lived before entering the monastery was dead now, too. Besides, from all he had heard, the plague was even worse in the crowded city than at the monastery.

No, if he wanted to escape this awful pestilence he would have to head in the opposite direction, higher into the hills. The monks talked of another monastery in the valley beyond. Perhaps it was free of the plague. If so, he might be able to join the brotherhood there and continue his studies in peace. He got to his feet, adjusted his cloak, and braced himself to face the wind again. Just then he heard the sound of a branch cracking behind the shelter. Was someone coming?

Anthony peered around the corner of the shelter and saw a shadow moving along the path. There was no way he could escape now without being seen. He would have to think of something to say to whomever it was — some excuse for having left his post in the infirmary without permission. He was still trying to find the right words when he heard a familiar voice.

"Anthony?" It was Brother Paul, on his way back to the monastery after burying the old woman in a common grave.

Embarrassed, Anthony nodded his head but said nothing.

"What are you doing here?"

"I — I — " Anthony could think of no plausible reason.

"Is anyone tending the infirmary?"

"No — I don't know." Anthony turned away toward the pond. He couldn't bear to face Brother Paul and the fierce look in his eyes.

The older monk took hold of Anthony's arm. "Then you must return at once."

"No!" Anthony blurted. "I can't go back there!"

"What do you mean? Of course you'll go back. It's your duty." Brother Paul kept his voice low, but his words had an icy firmness.

"I won't!" Anthony wailed. He didn't want to sound like a child, but he couldn't help it. "There's nothing but death there! I don't want to die!"

Brother Paul reached out and grasped the young man's shoulders. For a moment, Anthony thought the older monk was going to shake him. Instead, Brother Paul clasped him in a hug. "None of us wants to die," he said, and his voice was softer now. "But we can't allow our selfish worries to interfere with our duties to God — and to our fellow man."

Anthony felt the tension begin to leave his body. It had been a long time since anyone had hugged him. Before she died, his grandmother had occasionally given him a kiss on the cheek, but she was too frail for hugging. And the monks rarely showed affection to one another; they were too busy praying and studying and working in the fields. Or looking after the sick.

Anthony relaxed his head against Brother Paul's shoulder and let out an immense sigh. "I'm so afraid," he whispered. As he spoke the words, he realized that was exactly what the boy in the infirmary had said to him.

"We all are," Brother Paul replied gently, "but we can't let our fears keep us from our work." He drew back from Anthony. "Remember the psalm of David that we studied together last fall? 'The Lord is my light and my salvation; whom shall I fear?'"

"I remember," Anthony said, and he spoke the next words in the psalm: "'The Lord is the strength of my life; of whom shall I be afraid?'"

Brother Paul smiled. "My good pupil," he said. "But now you really must return to the infirmary. You're needed there."

Feeling calmer, Anthony looked up at the multitude of stars sprinkled like diamonds across the winter sky. Earlier, the boy had asked him a question many other people had been asking in the painful weeks since the plague had struck. Anthony had had no answer for the boy, because he was still seeking one for himself. Now he put the question to Brother Paul. "Does the plague mean the end of the world is near?"

Brother Paul put an arm around Anthony's shoulders, and together they studied the stars. "Only God knows the answer to that," the older monk said. "But I myself do not think it does. There is too much life in the world — new flowers and plants in the spring, a good harvest in the fall, babies all year round. I can't believe even this terrible pestilence can end all that."

As he listened to Brother Paul's words, Anthony let his gaze fall to the branches of a nearby tree. At first glance, the branches seemed frozen and bare. But if you looked at them closely, you could see the beginnings of new buds. Buds that soon would open into tender green leaves. It was just as Brother Paul had said — no matter how bleak the winter might be, spring would come again.

The older monk was still speaking. "Remember, too, that we're at the end of the millennium," he said.

"Mill-en-nium?" Anthony repeated slowly. From his studies he knew the word was Latin, but he didn't know what it meant.

"A thousand years," Brother Paul said.

Anthony still looked puzzled.

"You know we're living in the year of Our Lord 1000?" Brother Paul said patiently.

Anthony nodded.

"Well, next year will mark the start of a new millennium," the older monk said. "And I believe it will be a bright new beginning."

A millennium. A thousand years. Anthony found it almost impossible to imagine so long a span of time.

Brother Paul started to walk away, back toward the stone walls of the monastery. "Are you coming?" he asked Anthony.

The young monk hesitated for only a few seconds before saying yes. He took one last, long look at the starry heavens, then turned to follow Brother Paul. As they climbed the path that led to the monastery entrance, he asked the older monk, "What do you think life on earth will be like a thousand years from now?"

"I have no idea," Brother Paul said. "But you can be certain of one thing; it will be very different."

Anthony drew his cloak closer as if to protect himself from the horrors of the infirmary to which he was returning. "I wonder if people will have found a cure for plagues by then," he said.

Brother Paul held the heavy wooden door open for him. "We can hope they will, my brother," he said with a sigh. "We can hope."

The two monks walked down the corridor together, and Brother Paul stopped at the foot of the steps. "I'm going up to my cell," he said. For the first time Anthony detected a note of weariness in the older monk's voice. "Do you think you can take care of the patients by yourself until Brother Martin relieves you?"

Anthony nodded, then reached out impulsively to grasp the older monk's hand. "Thank you, Brother Paul," he said.

"For what?"

"For helping me to have faith again."

The infirmary was quiet when Anthony entered it and almost as cold as the yard outside. The fire in the brazier at the center of the room gave off little heat. Making his way by the light from a single, guttering candle, Anthony moved toward the cot where the boy lay.

Under the rough blanket, the boy's chest slowly rose and fell. He was still alive. Anthony sat on the edge of the cot, ready to tend to the boy's needs if he woke up. He was glad he had come back; as Brother Paul had said, he was needed here. And if the boy asked again whether the end of the world had come, Anthony would have an answer for him.

Author's Note

When Michael Cart invited me to submit a story for this anthology, I had my doubts at first. My writings had always centered on investigations of the past, not speculations about the future. But a sentence in Michael's letter made me think again: "Since these stories will have in common a concern for future issues, science/speculative fiction is certainly welcome; however, since we are what we were, retrospection might also be in order."

Retrospection . . . As I mulled over that word, I found myself traveling back in time and wondering how young people who were alive in A.D. *1000 responded to the advent of the second millennium. Were they excited by its prospects? Or were they fearful?*

From my research for such books as Be Seated

and When Plague Strikes, *I knew that in Western Europe, where my story is set, the year 1000 was a time of political and military strife. Wherever fighting occurred, epidemic diseases like bubonic plague were sure to follow. Christians everywhere feared that the end of the world and the Last Judgment were at hand.*

Monasteries similar to the one in the story were among the few places where people felt safe. After the collapse of the Roman Empire in the fourth and fifth centuries, monasteries had become the main centers of Western civilization. Besides offering religious instruction, they were also responsible for preserving the literature and learning of the ancients. If a plague broke out, sufferers often fled to the monasteries in search of medical care and treatment.

Anthony and Brother Paul are fictional characters, but I hope they will seem true to their times and themselves. More important, I hope young readers today will recognize in these long-ago monks some of their own thoughts and feelings at the start of another millennium.

STARRY, STARRY NIGHT

Michael Cart

Gazing up at the shining, star-encrusted sky that New Year's Eve was like looking at eternity — it seemed to go on forever. But it wouldn't. All of us gathered on the hilltop with our eyes glued to the sky knew it wouldn't. We knew because Noah had told us so, had told us that — at the last knell of midnight and the first moment of the new millennium — all of the stars we saw would start to wink out, one after another, until nothing remained for nonbelievers but the death of eternal darkness.

This was a super scary thought, and I moved closer to my girlfriend, Eve, for comfort. My hand found hers and held it. At that moment I felt more like a seven-year-old than a senior in high school. Eve squeezed my hand reassuringly, though, and smiled at me. As usual, she looked serene, almost beatific. She could have posed for a Renaissance painting of the Madonna. As for her father, Noah, the evangelist who had called us to the hilltop, he looked like the God that Michelangelo had painted on the ceiling of the Sistine Chapel. Or maybe, with his theatrically long gray hair, dramatic beard, and powerfully built body, it was the actor Charlton Heston in his Moses role that he resembled.

The TV cameras recording our hilltop assembly for a PBS documentary about the millennium added to the air of movie-of-the-week unreality. As if responding to a cue, Noah pointed a long forefinger at the sky. "In thirty minutes," he thundered, "the millennium will arrive and this sky shall pass away. But not before the heavens open to receive those of us who believe. DO you believe?" he demanded, the air trembling with the strength of his conviction.

"Yes!" the voices of his two hundred followers, Heaven's Elect, rapturously responded. And for a fleeting second, I felt as if I were attending a pep rally at school.

"Get a wide shot," one of the guys with the TV cameras ordered.

Without looking, Noah seemed to know exactly where the lenses were pointed. As I watched, I saw a red light wink on, and Noah smoothly dropped his right arm, which would have blocked the camera's view of his profile. He raised his left arm, instead, as he continued to goad the crowd, "God can't hear you if you whisper. DO YOU BELIEVE?"

"YES," the crowd roared.

"YES!" Eve cried.

"Yes," I whispered.

Until Noah and Eve had appeared in our small Northern California city the year before, I *had* been among those complacent nonbelievers who, Noah said, were about to be plunged into eternal darkness. It's not that I was an atheist; it was just that, like a lot of people, I'd been indifferent to religion most of my life — even though some of my earliest memories are of sitting in a hard church pew as I leaned contentedly against one of my parents and dozed while some man in a white robe droned on and on at the front of the sanctuary.

In fact, until I was five, my mom and dad had been conventional, card-carrying Christians who went to church two or three times a month, always taking me along.

All of that had changed, though, when Dad got cancer and Mom was helpless to do anything but watch him die, a process that took two years of unrelieved, unremitting agony. As for me — I didn't see my father at all the last three months of his life. He was in the hospital by then, and since I was only seven, the adults decided it would be too traumatic for me to see him there. Instead I saw his suffering embedded in Mom's face whenever she came home to rest. I always knew when he'd had an especially bad day by the look in her eyes. Toward the end, it got so bad that I couldn't bear to look at her at all.

I remember the day Dad died. Mom sat in the living room, calling people to tell them the news. I huddled timidly in the doorway behind her, hearing the word "dead" over and over; each time it was as if he had just died again. "How many times does he have to die?" I wanted to scream before I finally saw her put the phone back on its cradle after the last call. And I watched her shoulders heave as she began to sob.

And I remember how mad I was at God then for making my parents suffer.

As I grew up, though, the vividness of my memories faded like a photograph left in the sun, and gradually I forgot that I had once been angry at God.

But my mom didn't forget her anger. Remembering my dad's death turned her into someone you definitely wouldn't invite to a testimonial dinner for the Almighty.

Ten years after Dad died, Mom was still angry. But now it wasn't just God — and the religions that worshipped him — that she was mad at. It was a whole world of intolerance and injustice, of exploitation and inequity, of bad things happening to good people, of starlight being overwhelmed by darkness. . . .

"Listen to this," she would say each morning as I tried to eat my Wheaties in peace. And then she'd read aloud a newspaper account of what I had come to think of as "the daily atrocity." There was always at least one and some days so many it seemed that the whole world was engaged in a vast conspiracy to outrage my mom.

It was at the breakfast table that I first heard of Eve — well, of Noah actually. "Listen to this ad," Mom said, and from the paper read, "'Are you a True Believer? Find out by attending our Sunday service. Get right with God before the day of the millennium when, in His righteous wrath, He will destroy all unbelievers. Only the Elect of Heaven will be saved. Will you be among them?'

"And it's signed, 'Noah, Church of the New Heaven.'"
Mother snorted. "Talk about millennium madness!" She threw the paper down on the breakfast table. "God, I hope you never fall for something like this, Matthew."

Most kids are raised on dire warnings about the dangers of drugs. I must be one of the few who grew up hearing about the dangers of organized religion.

Mom recycled some of these warnings in her column, "Afflicting the Comfortable." It was syndicated to five hundred newspapers and was the reason she was also a regular talking head on PBS. Mom's outspoken opinions didn't make her very popular in our conservative small town. But because she was famous, people tended to look the other way. I mean, they didn't throw rocks at her or anything.

I wasn't so lucky. Oh, don't worry. People didn't stone me, either; they just shied away from me as if I were a leper — someone from whom they could catch the "disease" of Mom's left-leaning opinions. It made for a pretty lonely life and sometimes — well, sometimes, I guess, maybe I hated Mom for making me the local outcast.

Maybe that's why I fell head over heels in love with Eve — because she actually said hello the first time I saw her and gave me the gift of her beautiful smile. Ironically, it happened the same day that Mom read Noah's ad from the paper.

It must have been fate that assigned this beautiful stranger to my homeroom that mid-semester morning. Or maybe, as it turned out, God was playing a joke on Mom.

"Class," our teacher Miss Beatty said, "I want you to meet Eve Gates, our new student. Isn't she lovely?"

The new girl blushed. She was tall with cornflower blue eyes and hair the color of winter wheat.

Miss Beatty patted her hand. "Take any empty seat, dear," she said.

And that's when the miracle happened. Eve looked around the room and chose — actually *chose* — the seat next to mine. And that's when she said hello and smiled as she sat down. And that's when I fell — totally and hopelessly — in love with her.

I'm not sure if she loved me in return, but I do know that she loved God. I know because she told me so. She was sharing her beliefs with me less than an hour after we met. She even had a word for it: "witnessing." With anyone else, it would have been awkward and embarrassing, but with Eve, somehow it seemed as natural as sunshine. Of course, it helped that Mom had been talking about religion for as long as I could remember, so the subject was no stranger. And, too, Eve was a preacher's daughter, so you kind of expected it from her. But to most of the other kids she seemed weird, someone to shy away from the way they shied away from me. Which was pretty great, because it gave us another reason to hang out together. We were two outsiders who, when we were with each other, made our own inside.

I was glad, though, that Eve didn't ask me how *I* felt about God; not even after I told her who my mother was. Such questions were Noah's department, I guess. The very first time I met him, he looked at me with his X-ray eyes and demanded, "Are you right with God, young man? Or are you an enemy of the faith like your mother?"

Noah didn't waste a lot of time on polite how-do-you-dos, I would learn. He got right down to business, gathering souls for God.

"Time is short," he declared from the pulpit the first time I heard him preach, "the millennium is at hand. Those who are not with God are against Him and will feel the full weight of His wrath when that terrible, final day comes."

For the first time since I was five I found myself once again sitting in a hard pew on Sundays. Noah had rented an abandoned church and, with the help of a handful of his followers, had fixed it up as good as new. I had been among the fixer-uppers, and no one had worked harder than I had. At first my motivation had been selfishly simple: to demonstrate, with my sweat, that I wasn't the enemy, that I could be trusted to date Eve. But Noah had a way of complicating things. There was something so . . . *large* about him; something, some energy, some charisma, that made you want to please him. He had a natural talent for turning everybody into a little kid, clamoring for his attention. And when he gave it, when he first put his arm around my shoulder and said, of my work, "Good job, Son," I thought I had died and gone to heaven.

The need for Noah's approval was addictive and was one reason that no one was more faithful than I at attending Sunday worship services. When Noah caught your eye in mid-sermon and beamed approvingly at you, it was as if his big face were the sun descending into the sanctuary, warming you with its welcoming presence.

The other reason was sitting right next to me. It was Eve, whose hand I chastely held and whose calm beauty I worshipped out of the corner of my eye. And when Noah, angry at the congregation's lack of faith, withdrew his approval — as he did at least once every week — Eve was my island of serenity in the turbulent sea of words that her father's condemning voice was churning up.

As for Mom — she was making some waves, too.

"Have you taken leave of your senses, Matthew?" she demanded when I told her I was dating Eve. I hadn't intended to tell her so much — at least not right away — but I didn't have much choice after Eve and I ran into her at the mall and Mom demanded an introduction and, when I got home later, a full accounting. Then she threw a fit.

"But I like her, Mom," I protested, "I like her a lot. And besides, she's nice to me."

"Of course, she's nice to you; she's probably trying to brainwash you."

Eve threw a fit of her own the next day when I told her what Mom had said. It was the first time I'd seen her angry.

"Belief is not brainwashing," she said hotly. "And besides, what do you think your mother's trying to do in those columns of hers? Talk about the pot calling the kettle black."

No, I didn't tell Mom what Eve had said. And though I felt as guilty as hell, I didn't tell her where I was on Sunday mornings, either, while she was off in Sacramento appearing, thanks to a satellite feed, on a nationally televised PBS talk show. I wasn't exactly lying; I just wasn't telling the whole truth. I guess there's a difference.

After Mom's initial eruption, she didn't say too much. I suspect that she couldn't imagine that my relationship with the daughter of a fire-and-brimstone preacher would last. And so, after raising an eyebrow, she just said, "Well, I trust you not to do anything foolish." Which, of course, was her way of telling me not to do anything that she'd consider foolish. Like getting serious about Eve.

But it was too late. I *was* serious about Eve. In fact I was as obsessed with her as Noah was with God and the millennium. At least I didn't alert the media about it, though. . . .

"Millennialist Minister Predicts End of World" the headline in our local newspaper proclaimed several months later. The article that followed quoted Noah's dire predictions about the impending end of the world.

My mom peered at me over the top of the paper. "Are you still seeing that girl?" she asked.

"I dunno," I mumbled, staring at my cereal as if it were alphabet soup that could spell out the right answer.

"What do you mean, 'I dunno'?" Mom demanded.

I could feel her eyes boring into the top of my bowed head. She was looking at me the way she looked at the conservative politician who was point to her counterpoint on the PBS Sunday panel.

"All right, all right," I said. "Yes, I'm still dating her."

"What does she think about all of this?" Mom pointed to the headline.

"I guess she believes it," I said cautiously, and instantly felt like I was betraying Eve by diminishing her belief. Of course she believed it, and her belief was like a big boat in which she floated safely over the most turbulent seas of doubt.

Maybe that was why she always seemed so serene and why she was so easy to be with. Unlike my mom; being with her was like trying to ride out a typhoon of doubts, questions, and challenges in a leaky rowboat. It was exhausting, and sometimes downright terrifying. It was so much easier to be with Eve and with the rest of Heaven's Elect and to relax in the comfort of their unexamined beliefs.

"Uh-huh," Mom said relentlessly, going into her grand inquisitor mode, "and how do *you* feel about this end-of-the-world stuff?"

"I guess the world's got to end sometime."

"That's not what I mean, Matthew, and you know it. Do you believe that the world is going to come to an end on New Year's Eve?"

"I don't know, Mom," I said, trying not to feel cornered and failing. "I just know that's what Noah believes." And then, even though I knew it was childish, I couldn't resist adding, "Why do you hate him, anyway?"

"I don't hate him, Matthew," Mom said calmly, "I just think some of his claims are a bit . . . extravagant. And I'm not sure about his motivations."

"What do you mean?" I asked cautiously, not sure that I really wanted to know.

"I mean," she said, holding up the newspaper again, "he seems awfully interested in publicity."

"He's just trying to save souls," I protested.

"Maybe," Mom said, "but do you save souls by asking people to sign over their property to you?"

There was a moment of stunned silence. I should have been used to Mom's bombshells by now, I'd seen her toss so many on TV. But they always caught me by surprise, and I could never hide my shock.

"Oh, honey," she said, seeing the look of it on my face. "I'm a journalist, remember? It's my job to ask questions. I've been talking to people in this man's congregation, and I feel sorry for them. They're people the world hasn't treated kindly. They're old and lonely and afraid. And he's taking advantage of them. First he scares them to death with his talk about the end of the world, and then he promises them they'll survive as some kind of special elect if they give him enough money or property. It may not be illegal, but it's certainly exploitative."

As Mom talked, I felt my face getting hotter and hotter. "I don't believe it," I burst out now. "Eve would never go along with that."

"Maybe she doesn't know what her father is doing," Mom said.

"Or maybe *she* believes in him," I said.

Mom looked at me for a long minute before saying, "Maybe she does." Then she put her hand on mine. "But maybe it might be a good idea not to see quite so much of her."

It was a suggestion, not an order. But I pulled my hand away, nevertheless.

And I kept on seeing Eve. *What harm could it do?* I reasoned. I didn't have any property to sign over to her. All I had was my heart — and I'd already given her that.

But at least I did start paying closer attention to Noah's pronouncements from the pulpit. After Mom dropped her bombshell, I realized I had remained a five-year-old when it came to church; I was still leaning comfortably against the supportive love of the person next to me and ignoring the message that was supposed to be the thing I was there to hear.

And when I began to truly hear it, I was surprised — and, okay, dismayed — to discover that for someone who believed the world was about to end, Noah did seem awfully interested in money.

"Money is like blood," he roared from the pulpit. "Just as blood circulates through our bodies carrying life with it, so money circulates through the body of our affairs. But what is ours — whether it be life or money — is not ours to keep; it is a loan from God who expects that it shall be repaid . . . with interest. Do you doubt this? Are you skeptical? Or are you simply greedy, desiring to keep God's gifts for yourself? Then be afraid. Be very afraid. For your days are numbered. There is a place in the pit of eternal darkness with your name on it. But if you hear my words and believe them, if you then give freely back to God that which he has loaned to you — that and more — then even more abundant life will be yours. What God will give back to you then is a reserved seat in the New Earth and the New Heaven that will replace this earth, this place of plague and pestilential sin."

"Hallelujah!" an old man seated in front of me quavered.

"Yes," Noah said. "Hallelujah, indeed, and praise to God for choosing you. And what better way for you Elect to thank Him than with your generous offerings as the ushers now pass among you with collection plates."

I shifted in my seat, and Eve, sensing my discomfort, turned and smiled at me. And I was reassured . . . until I looked around at the congregation, at all the threadbare old people like the man in front of me, and at the others who looked as if life had beaten them half to death and then tossed them aside. They were looking at Noah as if HE were the Second Coming, and when the old collection plate came around, they gave until it hurt. At least it hurt me watching it, because it was another painful reminder of Mom's words, and not even another smile from Eve could reassure me now.

* * *

Nevertheless, when New Year's Eve arrived, there I was with Eve, standing atop the hill at the edge of town where Noah's Elect were gathered to be saved from the End.

"I'm sorry about your mother," Eve murmured.

"Why?" I asked.

"Because she doesn't have our faith. And because she won't be saved." I winced and Eve grabbed my hand. "Oh, Matthew," she said, "I'm so sorry."

She thought I was concerned about my mom's lack of faith. But that wasn't it at all. I was concerned that she might find out that mine was starting to crumble.

And now, as if they could read my thoughts, the TV crew turned their lights on again, and the anchor, a handsome man with white hair and a black suit, said to the camera, "The millennium — the dawn of a new age of belief or the death of reason?"

I figured Noah would have a fit when he found out his end-of-the-world party was going to be crashed by a horde of nonbelievers with TV cameras. But he seemed unconcerned. "Let them come," he had said when their van showed up earlier that evening. "What difference does it make? Who will watch their program when the final darkness comes?"

So why, I wondered, *was he now stepping into the camera's circle of light with a microphone pinned to his robe?* I looked at Eve quizzically, but like the crowd of the watching Elect, she only had eyes for her father.

"We are talking with Noah, founder of the Church of the New Heaven," the anchorman told an unseen audience. He turned to Eve's father. "Is it true," he asked, "that you believe the world will end at midnight?"

"Of course," Noah said, as if the answer were obvious.

"A thousand years ago at the time of the first millennium, there were many like you who prophesied the end of the world, and yet it's still here. So how do you know that it will end this time?" the anchorman pressed him. "Did God tell you?"

"I know what I know," is all that Noah would say. But he sounded so supremely self-confident that there was a scattering of applause from Heaven's Elect. It was led by Eve, who, I noticed, was now looking at her father with something like adoration. And to my surprise, this annoyed me — maybe because I wanted to be the one she looked at that way.

While I was thinking this, the anchorman was continuing his interview.

"And what will happen to you and your congregation when the world ends?"

"We will be taken to heaven," Noah replied.

"In an ark?" the anchorman asked eagerly. "Have you built an ark?"

"The Biblical Noah was subjected to scorn like yours," Noah said sternly. "But he had the last laugh when the deluge came."

"I see," the anchorman said. He paused for a moment and then, with a great show of sincerity, said, "Help me to understand this. Why, exactly, is God going to destroy the earth?"

"'And God saw that the wickedness of man was great in the earth, and that every imagination of the thoughts of his heart was only evil continually.'"

I recognized the Bible verse. It was one that Noah often quoted.

To my surprise the anchorman supplied the next verse, "But Noah found grace in the eyes of the Lord."

Noah smiled like someone running for office. "I know you're being sarcastic," he said, "but, in truth, I feel that God has visited His grace on me and on the Elect of Heaven who are gathered here in faith. Understand that after God has destroyed this world, there will be a new heaven and a new earth, and we have been chosen, like the first Noah and his family, to replenish it." He sounded like he was having a wonderful time.

The anchorman paused as if he were mentally shifting gears and then, "In a nationally syndicated column that will be published tomorrow," he said, "the well-known writer and television personality Margaret Fuller writes — and I quote — 'If you're reading this, the world has not ended after all, despite the claims of a small-town millennialist named Noah, a man who has managed to garner publicity for himself by making outrageous claims that a fire-and-brimstone God will destroy the earth and all of its population on New Year's Eve — except, of course, for himself and his followers. And the sad thing is that there are people who are so frightened and so desperate to belong somewhere that they believe this.'"

My stomach suddenly felt as if it were in an elevator that was descending too far, too fast. For the first time, some of Noah's followers were looking at me and shrinking away, just like the kids at school did. I didn't dare even to glance at Eve for fear I would see her doing the same.

"What do you say to this?" the anchorman asked.

There was a terrible silence that was finally broken by Noah's voice . . . saying my name.

"Matthew," it called, "Matthew, come here."

Oh, God, I thought. I knew now that something terrible was going to happen, but I didn't yet know what. And so I hung back like a little kid pretending he doesn't hear his parent's voice calling him to a punishment for some transgression.

But then, "Matthew," a new voice called, joining Noah's in the summons, "Matthew."

It was Eve. And this time I did look at her, to see her sweet, reassuring smile. "Noah needs you," she said and, slipping her arm through mine, gently led me to the circle of light that surrounded her father.

She stepped into the circle with me as Noah put a big arm around my shoulders and drew me close to him.

"Do you know who this boy is?" he asked the anchor.

But he didn't wait for an answer. "This" — he paused for one exquisite moment like a gambler preparing to reveal his trump card — "this is Matthew Fuller."

The anchorman looked bewildered.

"Matthew Fuller," Noah said, "is Margaret Fuller's son. And he is one of us."

"Is that true?" the anchorman asked. It was me he was talking to and looking at. And for the first time I became acutely aware that I — like Eve and the other Elect — was wearing a pristinely white robe. It seemed to be a spotlight illuminating me for the whole world to see. I felt awkward and foolish, and I found myself wondering what Mom would think when she saw me on TV.

"Tell him," Noah said, and the weight of his arm around my shoulders that had once felt so reassuring now felt immense and crushing.

"Tell him," Eve echoed, her arm still slipped through mine. Her sweet persistence was getting on my nerves, I realized. She was starting to sound like a mother assuring her gullible child that there are no monsters under the bed.

But I knew different: There are monsters, horrible ones. And here they come, I thought, as I opened my mouth to whisper, "Yes, I'm Matthew Fuller."

"God can't hear you if you whisper," Noah chided, squeezing my shoulder as, with practiced efficiency, he removed the microphone from his collar and placed it in front of my mouth.

"And neither, apparently, can my audience," the anchorman said, an odd smile curling his lips.

This time Noah didn't wait for a question to speak. "I have called Matthew Fuller to join me here so that people can see, with their own eyes, his physical presence. And to see in that presence a repudiation of his mother's empty words and the manifestation of his own belief, which is a denial of her doubts."

The crowd of the Elect burst into applause.

"Wait," the anchorman ordered. "Let the boy speak for himself."

Everyone's eyes shifted now from Noah to me. I glanced at Eve, whose eyes smiled encouragement. And I looked away. Did she really expect me to betray my own mother?

"Well, Matthew," the anchorman said briskly, "do you agree with Noah? Is your presence a — let me see if I can remember his sermon — a 'repudiation' of your mother's 'empty words,' and is your belief a 'denial of her doubts'?"

A week ago it would have been so easy to answer yes, so easy to relax into the sweet comfort of Eve's acceptance and Noah's approval. To say what they wanted to hear. To add words to the betrayal of my mom that my silent, un-questioning presence had been. Yes, even I understood — now that I had been dragged in front of the cameras by Noah — that my presence had been an implicit betrayal.

And — I almost laughed now — I also finally understood that all those Sundays while I had been basking in the warmth of Noah's approval, he had been coldly planning to use me. Mom had been right about him. But what about Eve? Had she also been using me to betray my mom and everything that she believed in?

I looked at her and I sighed, exhaling with the breath some part of me that, for a while, had made such a difference. I hadn't wanted a place in heaven. All I had wanted was a place in Eve's heart. That would have been heaven enough for me. But it wasn't to be. Her heart wasn't big enough to hold her belief and me.

I sighed again and said the words I now knew I had to say, "No. I don't agree."

Eve flinched as if I had slapped her, and I felt Noah's arm fall away from my shoulders.

"I'm sorry," I said, wondering if even the end of the world could hurt this bad. I was looking at the anchorman, but I was speaking to Eve. "I don't belong here. I don't believe. I'm so sorry."

It was then, as if my words had been a signal, that the sky began to explode.

People screamed and, like cattle in a thunderstorm, began milling wildly about. "It's the end!" I heard someone scream, and realized it was Eve. The sky was suddenly on fire and split with the sounds of explosions and of shouted prayers and oaths. And then in the middle of it all time seemed to stop, freezing action. Reason tilted crazily on its axis as my mind tried desperately to make sense of it all, and in that endless, frozen moment I had forever to look at Noah's face and at the expression on it: a look of absolute astonishment.

But then, mercifully, reality returned, and time resumed its relentless ticking.

"Be calm, people," the anchorman bellowed, "it's just fireworks."

The Elect of the New Heaven stopped in their tracks and raised their eyes to the drama in the sky. And suddenly everyone knew exactly what it signified.

The anchorman was already explaining it to one of his cameras. "The brilliant fireworks display marks the arrival of midnight and, with it, a new millennium. And if there were any lingering doubts, it is now obvious that despite Noah's predictions, the same old world is still here to welcome it."

He turned to Noah. The look of surprise was gone from the preacher's face — if it had ever been there at all — replaced by his usual air of commanding authority.

"Do you feel betrayed by God? Are your beliefs shaken?" the anchorman asked.

"Of course not," Noah said without a pause, as if his remarks had been rehearsed. "God is testing our belief, that's all. And I guarantee you, he will not find us wanting. Am I right?" he demanded. His followers, who had gathered around him, burst into applause — led, of course, by Eve, the look of serenity once again locked securely on her face.

They all seemed to have forgotten that I was there. I stepped out of the circle of light, slipped the robe over my head, and dropped it to the ground. It was the same old world, all right. Noah and Eve still knew what they believed. Mother still knew what she believed. But me? Well, it was a new year, and, to my surprise, I found myself thinking that maybe it was time for me to go home and try to figure out for myself what *I* believed.

I looked up. The fireworks had faded away by now, and once again I could see the sky encrusted with countless, shining stars. Maybe they wouldn't last forever. But there they had been for millennia, and I found I could believe at least one thing already: I could believe they would be there at least long enough to light my way home.

I smiled up at them wistfully and started to make my way there.

Author's Note

Every Sunday, when I was a boy growing up in Indiana in the 1940s, my mother took me and my sister to Sunday school and church. I remember being fascinated by the almost actorlike performance of our pastor as he led the congregation in worship. His sermons were my first exposure to the power and the drama of the spoken word. Years later, when I had grown up and moved to California, I saw television evangelists for the first time and was even more intrigued by the mesmerizing power they exerted over their audiences. What would have happened to me if I had encountered one of them when I was a lonely teenager? *I wondered.* Might I have ended as a true believer in a Jonestown or a Waco? *It was such speculation that inspired the story "Starry, Starry Night."*

About the Authors

JON SCIESZKA, who worked as an elementary school teacher for many years, came to write children's books by "hanging out with second graders." Best known for his parodies of fairy tale classics (*The True Story of the Three Little Pigs, The Stinky Cheese Man, The Frog Prince Continued,* etc.), he is also the author of the Time Warp Trio series and, most recently, the fractured retellings of Aesop's fables, *Squids Will Be Squids.* He lives with his family in Brooklyn, New York.

RODMAN PHILBRICK grew up on the New England coast, where he worked as a longshoreman and boatbuilder. For many years he wrote mysteries and thrillers for adults. Then, inspired by the life of a boy who lived a few blocks away, he wrote *Freak the Mighty,* the award-winning young adult novel. The book was adapted for the screen as *The Mighty.* He's also the author of *The Fire Pony, Max the Mighty,* and *REM World,* as well as many mass-market books for young readers, cowritten with his wife, Lynn Harnett. Rod and Lynn divide their time between Maine and the Florida Keys.

TOR SEIDLER grew up in Vermont and Seattle, Washington. After graduating from Stanford University, he moved briefly to Boston, then to New York City, where he's lived ever since. He's had a variety of jobs, ranging from waiting on tables to teaching, but most of his energy has gone into writing. To date he's written eight novels for children, including *A Rat's Tale, The Wainscott Weasel, Mean Margaret* (a National Book Award finalist), and, most recently, *The Silent Spillbills.* He has also written for adults, one novel published and one just completed.

RON KOERTGE is the author of eight acclaimed novels, including *The Arizona Kid,* selected by the American Library Association as one of the top one hundred young adult novels published since 1967. Also an award-winning poet, he lives in Southern California, where he is a professor of English at Pasadena City College.

GLORIA SKURZYNSKI is the author of forty books for young readers, including the science fiction novels *Cyberstorm* and *Virtual War* and the recent nonfiction book *Discover Mars.* She has received many national awards for both fiction and nonfiction; in 1992 she won the American Institute of Physics science writing award. Her web site is *http://redhawknorth.com/gloria*

LOIS LOWRY, who has worked as a journalist and photographer, is the author of twenty-five books for young readers, including the popular Anastasia Krupnik series. She has received countless honors, including the *Boston Globe-Horn Book* Award, the Dorothy Canfield Fisher Award, and two Newbery Medals for her novels *Number the Stars* and *The Giver.* Her most recent book is the autobiographical *Looking Back.* She divides her time between Massachusetts and an 1840s farmhouse in rural New Hampshire.

KATHERINE PATERSON is the author of more than twenty-five books, including twelve novels for young people. Two of these novels are National Book Award winners, *The Master Puppeteer,* 1977, and *The Great Gilly Hopkins,* 1979, which was also the single Honor Book for the 1979 Newbery Medal. She received the Newbery Medal in 1978 for *Bridge to Terabithia* and again in 1981 for *Jacob Have I Loved. Lyddie* was the U.S. contribution to the Honors List of the International Board of Books for Young People in 1994, and *Jip, His Story,* was the winner of the 1997 Scott O'Dell Award for Historical Fiction. Her books have been published in twenty-two languages, and she was the 1998 recipient of the most distinguished international award given for contributions to children's literature, the Hans Christian Andersen Medal.

JACQUELINE WOODSON is the author of a number of novels, including *If You Come Softly, The House You Pass on the Way,* and the Coretta Scott King Honor Books *I Hadn't Meant To Tell You This* and *From the Notebooks of Melanin Sun.* She lives in Brooklyn, New York.

JAMES CROSS GIBLIN is the author of eighteen nonfiction books, many of which have won awards and honors. Twelve of his titles, most recently *Charles A. Lindbergh: A Human Hero,* have been named Notable Children's Books by the American Library Association. In 1996 he received the *Washington Post*-Children's Book Guild Award for Nonfiction for the body of his work. Recently Mr. Giblin ventured into fiction. He contributed a short story to the anthology *Am I Blue? Coming Out From the Silence* and wrote a picture book based on an Arthurian tale, *The Dwarf, the Giant, and the Unicorn.*

MICHAEL CART was, for a number of years, director of the Beverly Hills Public Library. Since 1991, however, he has been a full-time writer, lecturer, and consultant. He is the author of four books, including the novel *My Father's Scar,* which was a 1997 ALA Best Book for Young Adults. His column, "Carte Blanche," appears monthly in *Booklist* magazine.